2014

#104

Finding Joshua

A Stand-Alone Romance Novel

F/BU

Romance Novel

By

Pamela Bush

Pamela Bush
I Cor. 15:58

Finding Joshua

Published September 2014 by Pamela Bush

This novel is a work of fiction. Even though actual locations are mentioned – names descriptions, entities, and incidents included in the story are amplified products of the author's imagination. Any resemblance to actual persons and entities is entirely coincidental.

Cover Design by TJ Grant

www.tjgrant.net

Published in the United States of America

ISBN: 978-0-9848036-2-0

     1. Fiction: Christian: Romance

     2. Fiction: Christian: Fantasy

Pamela Bush

What People Say about Pamela Bush's books:

WHIRLWIND FICTION SERIES:

*"I started reading **Out of the Whirlwind** and didn't stop until I read it cover to cover. I've shared this book with several friends. We all want to read more, so I plan to buy the other two books." - Sheryl T.*

"You are a gifted writer. He has blessed you with compassion, insight, knowledge, and wisdom on how to apply it all." - Emma K.

*"**Out of the Whirlwind** is a book that would help anyone going through a difficult time!" – Tressa*

*"Pamela Bush weaves together a spellbinding novel of crime, passion, and romance with a powerful message of redemption and hope in the midst of life's tragedies in **Out of the Snare**." - Edward E.*

"Out of the Snare is an exceptional piece of literary art that keeps one intrigued page by page." – Laura T.

*"I've been wanting to purchase **Out of the Snare**, but it hasn't worked out; then I went to my Mom's and she had one sitting on the table. A friend had loaned it to her. I started reading it and couldn't put it down!" - Deb H.*

*"**Out of the Mire** is hard to put down. This is my favorite one of the trilogy." - Doug B.*

"**Out of the Mire** *starts out like a harlequin, but soon picks up. I couldn't put it down. In fact, I stayed up until 12:30 p.m. to finish it – which is late for me! - Della B.*

AUTHOR'S FIRST NON-FICTION NOVEL:

"**The Fire Within: Fighting Through Adversity** *is a book that I will read again! It's written in a way that is believable and yet, makes you wonder how Paul and his wife Gretchen remained married with everything that came at them. I would recommend this book to ANYONE who's going through adversity – - whatever form that may be." - Judi B.*

"*Wow! I can't believe how good* **The Fire Within: Fighting Through Adversity** *is. Paul Bush truly has the Spirit of God helping him throughout his life. It's amazing the experimental things that he's gone through. The cement beads doused with antibiotics was a new one to me."*
- Nurse Gwyn N.

"*My dad just finished the book:* **The Fire Within: Fighting Through Adversity** *and really enjoyed it. He is sharing it with a friend, and then maybe I'll get it back so I can read it too! - Darcie G.*
"*Finished The Fire Within: Fighting Through Adversity and am so thankful that you wrote it. Very touching. Your family is blessed!" - Amanda E.*

This book is dedicated to

my Mother-in-love,

Della Bush.

Thank you for loving me and making

me a part of your family.

And, for giving us the photo

that prompted the fun writing of this story.

**Thank you Jesus for being
my Lord and Savior!
Without You, I couldn't cope with the rapid
way the world is changing around me.**

*I Corinthians 15:58:
"Therefore, my beloved brethren, be steadfast,
immovable, always abounding in the work of the
Lord, knowing that your labor is not in vain in
the Lord."*

CHAPTER ONE

Elizabeth Warner held the small stack of photos tightly as she stared out the car windshield. The snow drifts were crowding the road more rapidly than just a few minutes earlier and she was beginning to fret.

Right then the car skimmed another drift forming across the road with the onslaught of snow and wind. Pulling her eyes left, Elizabeth worriedly said to her husband, "Josh, the wind is blowing harder now and we still have a good half hour drive yet. Do you think we should turn around and head back to your Mom's? It's closer than our place."

Joshua Warner ran one hand through his wavy, greying dark hair while assuring, "Liz, we've driven in this kind of weather all our lives. It'll be fine. Another mile down the road we could drive right out of it into sunshine." Flashing a confident smile, he touched her hand briefly before grabbing the steering wheel as another snow drift tugged the car.

Reassured by his calmness, Liz relaxed. Focusing once again on the photos held in her hands, Liz's mind promptly traveled back in time. "Hey, remember when we were first married and we owned that orange super Beetle VW?"

"Sure I do. I loved that car. It was the first brand new vehicle I'd ever bought!"

Allowing her mind to continue down memory lane, Liz then asked, "Remember how you used to love busting snowdrifts with it?" Getting more excited, she added, "And . . . remember? We used to drive it in State Land."

Shooting her a loving look, Joshua replied, "Yup. We'd go everywhere the dirt bikes went." A reflective silence followed as images of steep hills and narrow spaces coursed through both of their minds.

"It was great times," Josh said, and then added with a heavy sigh, "but it seems so long ago."

Sitting straighter, Liz said enthusiastically, "Speaking of long ago, I love these photos your Mom just gave us." She thumbed through them, but stopped at one in particular. Pulling it from the stack, she held it up to study more intently. "How old are you in this one? And where were you?"

She positioned the photo closer to Josh's line of vision.

"Um, let's see . . . that was the summer of my senior year in high school. We were living in Louisiana and some friends had come for a visit. That day my parents, brother and I had taken the four of them to tour the French Quarters of New Orleans."

Liz pulled the photo back to peer at it more closely. She wanted to better study this younger, more virile version of her beloved husband. The photo consisted of eight people standing in the vicinity of an old antique shop with wire mesh cages protecting the store front windows. Above one window on the right was a dangling sign. Liz could almost feel a soft breeze swinging it back and forth as she read the words: *Royal Trash and Treasures*. *What a unique and interesting name for an antique store!* Four older people were standing on the right of the photo under the sign, while Josh's brother and two unknown girls wearing skirts were further down the sidewalk, to the left. Liz decided the shop was obviously large, for the threesome was peering into one of the mesh windows of the same store.

Her Joshua was in the middle of the photo. It looked like he'd just left the older group and was now walking toward the younger.

Liz strained to see his hazel eyes, but couldn't quite make them out. Instead, she focused on his overall physical shape. "You look absolutely great in this photo! Your dress slacks ... short sleeved shirt ... neat haircut, and ... buffed up body!"

Joshua chuckled at the tone of her voice, but concentrated on his driving. The snow was letting up, but now they were passing over patches of slippery ice on the road. *Just fifteen more minutes and we'll be safely home.*

Beside him, Elizabeth let out a heavy sigh. "You and I didn't meet until almost seven years after this photo was taken. I wish I could have known you then. Do you think you'd have noticed me?"

"I noticed you in 1972 at your sister's wedding in Michigan, so why wouldn't I have done the same the summer of 1965 in Louisiana?" He paused a moment before stating with a grin, "Although I must admit your long auburn hair definitely caught my eye back then, where now it's just above your shoulder in length . . . and, I might add becoming sprinkled with lovely shades of gray."

Liz raised one eyebrow at his comment. Choosing to ignore it, she shrugged. "I don't know; times were different back then."

A short laugh came out of Joshua before he stated, "Back then, Lizzie? There's only six years between us." Not receiving a reply, Joshua changed the subject by mentioning that the snowfall seemed to be letting up. Just as he had previously predicted. Still not getting anything out of Elizabeth, he pulled his eyes from the road to briefly glimpse her head leaned back against the rest with eyes closed. The photo held close to her heart.

"Lizzie . . . knowing the creative mind you have, are you by chance daydreaming of being in that photo?" he asked with a teasing tone to his voice.

Out of the corner of his eye, Joshua saw red tinge her cheeks as Liz's head abruptly came up.

"Yes, I was." She replied a little defensively. "I was trying to imagine myself back there and what could have happened between us."

She paused and then said, "Josh, there were two girls with you and your brother. How do you know if I happened to walk by that you'd notice me?"

"Sweetheart . . . as I already stated . . . I definitely noticed you in Michigan; with your long auburn hair, freckles, and deep blue eyes. Trust me. There's no way I wouldn't have noticed you back in the time of that photo." He then added with a tease, "Besides your light Scandinavian complexion would clearly stand out down there."

Smiling, Joshua again briefly pulled his eyes from the road to flash her a loving look. "And just to let you know, those girls didn't mean . . ." Joshua never got to finish his sentence, because right then something caught his attention over Liz's right shoulder.

Elizabeth saw his eyes dilate with fear and horror. The next second his arm swung out to smash her body violently against the car seat. Staring anxiously at his face, she heard him exclaim, "God….be merciful!"

Then everything went into slow motion, as Liz heard metal hitting metal, the car begin moving sideways, mixed with a fleeting image of photos scattering. She heard a scream, felt horrific pain, and then everything went black.

A short time later, the blackness turned into . . . warmth, bright sunlight and bodies bumping into her . . . followed by lots and lots of confusion.

CHAPTER TWO

Elizabeth wasn't sure where she was – or where she'd been.

Everything at first was fuzzy, but as more and more people nudged or bumped her, Liz finally was able to get clarity; only to find herself standing on a sidewalk. *A somewhat busy sidewalk . . . in a city? What on earth?*

Elizabeth rubbed her head and eyes trying to make sense of it all. It was then she realized her glasses were missing. *Great! That's just what I need!*

As she bent down to search the sidewalk for them, a long auburn ponytail fell forward. Momentarily forgetting the glasses, she straightened as another passing person bumped her. Mesmerized, she studied the golden hued hair in her hand. It gave off a beautiful glow as the sun's rays hit it. A vision of much shorter hair kept playing with her mind; but was pushed aside when another reality hit her. *I can see perfectly well without my glasses.* Feeling her face once more to verify the glasses were indeed missing, Liz marveled at her perfect vision. Knitting her brows, she wondered out loud, "What's going on?"

Thoroughly confused, she tried desperately to make sense of what was happening. Raising her eyes, Liz forced herself to study the surroundings as her heart began to race. "Take a deep breath, Liz, and calm down. This can be explained." She inhaled deeply and exhaled slowly. It helped steady her rapidly rising pulse, but didn't clear up any of the confusion.

Okay . . . let's see what I do know. I know my name is Elizabeth, and . . . I have no idea where I am . . . or why. Think Elizabeth – think! You're obviously in a city and it's hot out, so it must be summer. Panic began seeping into her being once more as she just couldn't get a handle on what was going on. Forcing herself to calm, Elizabeth took a few moments to study the street and surroundings. To her surprise, they seemed somewhat familiar, but in a vague, just learned sort of way; more like an eerie deja vu kind of thing.

The fact she was still standing in the middle of the sidewalk, finally infiltrated Liz' muddled brain enough to cause her to consider moving out of the foot traffic. Swinging around, she spied a building nearby that would offer her a somewhat safer haven, but before Liz could take a step a masculine voice spoke at her elbow.

"Are you alright? You seem confused."

Relieved at hearing Joshua's voice, Elizabeth smiled and turned to look slightly up into his warm hazel eyes; but then the confusion came back in full force. It was her Joshua's voice but instead of seeing a man in his early sixties, she was standing in front of a young man in his late teens.

Elizabeth found herself staring as his eye color deepened and a frown creased his brows. Pulling her mind back to his words, she considered his question then slowly replied, "Yes…I think I'm okay. I just got a little confused for a moment there. I thought you were someone else."

Studying her more closely, he asked, "Did you hit your head or something?"

Briefly examining herself all over, Liz replied, "I don't think so."

Realizing she may be drawing attention, Elizabeth felt a blush cross her cheeks as she hurriedly added, "Actually, I'm feeling much better now." Right then she became aware of the sun hitting her and came up with a possible excuse for her apparent state of confusion, "Maybe the heat just got to me a little bit."

The young man's face clearly expressed doubt at her explanation, but offering a hand he suggested, "Maybe you need to sit down and drink something cool. You know – rest a minute."

Growing increasingly uncomfortable with his questions and concern, Liz replied a bit testier than she intended. "That's a nice idea, but where do you suggest I do this?" She hoped he'd be turned off by her rudeness and walk away.

Instead, he smiled, placed a hand on her elbow and turned her to look behind her. There just a few feet away was a small sidewalk café covered by a checked awning. Keeping his hand on her elbow, he gently, but expertly guided her towards the nearest vacant table.

Right then a female voice rang out, "Hey, Joshua. Where are you going? You said you'd spend the day with us."

Glancing over her shoulder, Liz noted the words came from a girl standing beside a young man and another girl in front of a large wire mesh covered storefront window. Feeling deja vu again, Liz's eyes traveled further down the block to see a metal arm holding a swaying sign which read: Royal Trash and Treasures.

She froze. *Why does all of this seem so familiar and yet so strange?*

A feeling of panic started to swell within her, until she felt a firm hand squeeze her elbow. Glancing sideways, Liz became acutely aware of the young man standing at her side. By the look on his face, he'd seen her expressions, for his now sported a determined look. Ignoring the female voice, he pulled out a white wrought iron chair while stating in a slightly, raised voice, "You guys go on. I'll catch up in a bit."

He waited for Liz to take a seat, then positioned himself across from her at the small metal table. The concerned look remained in his eyes as he studied Elizabeth's face. "You're still a little pale. Maybe something cold will help."

As if on cue, a waiter walked up and two glasses of ice tea with lemon were ordered.

An awkward silence ensued as the two took stock of each other. Liz openly studied the young man across from her. He looked to be about college age and was neatly dressed with black slacks and a forest green short sleeved shirt that was tight enough around his upper arms to accentuate firm muscles. His hair was just shy of a military cut and seemed to be appropriate for the heat of the day. His whole demeanor spoke relaxed and calm. It occurred to her that he was the type you'd want around during a time of crisis. *Like now?* She thought with a heavy sigh, and then jumped when he spoke.

"A little jumpy, huh?" Seeing she didn't mean to respond, he continued. "From your accent, I'd say you're from the north somewhere."

"Michigan." That prompt reply caused Elizabeth to pause and think, *strange I knew that.* She mulled that answer over a bit and knew within, that it was right. *I am from Michigan!* Before she could further speculate things about herself, Liz was brought back to the present and the young man seated near her. It distressed Elizabeth that she had a strong sense that she should know this young man, but for the life of her she couldn't pull up who he was. Instead, she was stuck in the strange feeling of déjà vu.

Her answer had apparently stirred some interest, because he was now leaning forward to enthusiastically say, "Really? I spent my elementary years there; then the beginning of high school we moved down here."

Shrugging, he added, "It's where Dad could find work."

At that point, the waiter returned with the tea. Feeling suddenly parched, Liz took a long drink, ignoring the fact that it was sweetened. Growing embarrassed over gulping the tea, Liz set it down, wiped her mouth with a nearby napkin, and then began playing with the moisture condensing on the side of her glass. She intended to say thank-you for his kindness, but instead heard herself blurt, "Have we met before? There's something very familiar about you. . . ."

"No, I've never met you before." She noted his head tilt and eyes dance as he added in a lower voice, "Believe me . . . I'd have remembered you. Your lovely auburn hair, freckles and blue eyes aren't easily forgotten." He shook his head for emphasis.

If her face had been pale, Elizabeth knew it wasn't now as a blush stole up her neck and cheeks. Fumbling her words, she hurriedly said, "Well, thank you for your help." Tilting her own head, she added through lowered lashes, "You're a true southern gentleman."

She couldn't help but feel a bit of satisfaction, when a slight blush touched his masculine face.

Catching her eyes with his, he willed her to maintain eye contact as he asked, "So, at the risk of being forward, may I ask your name?"

"Elizabeth . . . Elizabeth." She stopped because the last name eluded her. To cover up, she hurriedly added, "But, my friends call me Liz or Lizzie."

With confidence, he stated, "Liz it is! I'm Joshua Warner, but I prefer Josh."

Extending her hand, Liz shyly said, "It's nice to meet you . . . Josh."

Holding hands a fraction longer than necessary, the two quickly dropped them when the female voice rang out again. "Joshua, we're going into the store now."

"Fine," he replied before turning back to the petite auburn haired girl seated across from him. "So, Liz . . . what are you doing in New Orleans?"

New Orleans! I'm in New Orleans? What am I doing here? Not having a clue as to why she was in Louisiana, Liz stated the first excuse that popped into her head. "I'm . . . uh . . . visiting family for the summer."

"That's great!" Realizing he probably sounded a little too enthusiastic, Joshua took a quick drink of tea.

For the first time, Elizabeth felt herself relax and grow even a little flirty. Cocking her head again, her auburn ponytail fell over her shoulder as she asked coyly, "Is it really a great thing?"

At that moment, something caught Joshua's attention off to her right.

Liz's eyes followed the direction he was looking and she noted four adults standing further down the block. One of the women was signaling Joshua. Elizabeth couldn't help from staring, for once again, she had the distinct feeling that she'd seen the scene before; and that she knew the woman. *But I have no memory of ever being in Louisiana before; nor of meeting any of these people . . . except maybe . . .* Something elusive kept niggling at her brain, but before she could concentrate further on what it could be, Joshua came to his feet and pulled out his wallet.

With a look of genuine regret he stated, "It looks like my parents are ready to leave, so I must go." Extracting some bills, he laid them on the table.

Growing flustered at his paying for the drinks, Elizabeth reached for her purse, but didn't find one. Frowning, she searched the area surrounding her, but didn't see a purse anywhere in sight.

"Did you lose something?"

She raised troubled eyes Joshua's way to observe that concerned look still on his face, but this time it was accompanied by one raised eyebrow. Quickly assessing the fact she didn't have any money, Elizabeth covered her further confusion with one of her best smiles and said, "No . . . no." He looked to say more, so she quickly added, "Thank you for the tea. It was very refreshing. I feel fine now."

His face still held doubt as to the accuracy of her statement, but Joshua didn't reply. Instead, he glanced at the four adults to his left and then at the trio emerging from the store nearby. He then leveled eyes her way to hurriedly say, "Listen . . . I was wondering if maybe I could give you a call. You know – show you the sights or something?"

Meeting his look head on, a still bewildered Liz wondered if she even had a number as she sincerely responded, "I'd like that." Stalling, she then asked, "Do you have paper to write on?"

"The napkin will do." Pulling a pen from his shirt pocket, Joshua held the pen poised for the number.

Elizabeth scrambled through the corners of her mind for a number. Feeling her face growing red, a sense of panic coursed through her veins until suddenly from out of the blue a number popped into her head. Elizabeth desperately tried to pull her inner chaos into a semblance of control while slowly stating the number to the kind, handsome young man standing before her.

Joshua scribbled the number down and then raised eyes still reflecting lingering concern for her wellbeing. He studied her face a seemingly long time before stating, "Okay, then. Take it easy in this hot Louisiana sun and I'll be calling."

With that he was gone and Elizabeth thoughtfully sipped her tea, while hoping the number would somehow bring the young man back into her life.

She watched him walk back to the four adults, then blushed when he briefly turned back and caught her. Liz quickly turned her eyes back to the drink in her hand and smiled. She had a feeling that somehow he was going to play a pivotal part in her life and the thought sent excitement coursing through her veins.

Closing her eyes she replayed the conversation, and then grew quiet as her senses began concentrating on the sounds flowing all around her. Voices floated by. High pitched females. Low voiced men. Car tires on the pavement. A baby crying; even a dog barking.

Then, off in the distance, Liz heard an ambulance siren. Tilting her head, she listened intently as the sound seemed to be getting closer, and closer. In fact, the sound seemed to pull up right next to her but when Elizabeth turned to look, there wasn't an ambulance in sight.

Sadly, Liz thought about all the accidents that happen every second around the world, plus she could vividly imagine all the people affected by those accidents. Coming to a stand she softly said, "When I hear sirens; either someone's suffering or . . . worse!"

With an effort, Liz cleared the depressing thoughts from her mind. *I'm not going to dwell on sad things – instead I choose to remember the warm hazel eyes of a handsome, kind young man who says he's going to call!*

Still – as Elizabeth walked away she wondered why a strong sense of dread still lingered.

~~~~~~~~~

"Man! What was that?"

"Someone blew the stop sign and broadsided a car!"

"I was in the gas station and it sounded awful! Many of us came running out."

"It was awful! I was pumping gas into my van and saw the whole thing! As far as I could tell the man in the four door hemi truck never even tried to slow down, let alone stop." Turning to the guy now standing beside him, the man questioned, "Did someone call the police?"

"I heard several on their cell phones as I ran out."

The men peered at the twisted metal wreckage a short distance away. The two vehicles were locked together in a weird embrace, with the car engine pushed up against a telephone pole.

"The good thing is - the road condition had the vehicles going slower than normal."

"I sure hope the truck driver wasn't drunk or texting! Otherwise they could be in big trouble."

"Me, too! But, you know, it very easily could have been a patch of ice."

"I hope there wasn't anybody on the passenger side. That looks to have taken most of the damage."

"If there was, hopefully it had a side air bag . . . well here they come!"

Right then a police car and ambulance pulled up and everyone jumped into action.

Suddenly, the younger man of the two observers pointed. "Would you look at that!"

The driver side door of the car opened and a man climbed out. The men watched him stagger then grip the car with his left hand. The right one seemed to dangle loosely at his side. An EMT woman ran to him as he partially collapsed against the car.

"I wonder if they called the fire department. If someone is on the other side of that car, they're going to need the Jaws of Life."

"Oh, oh! Look at the man."

At that moment, the man was desperately trying to get to the other side of the vehicle. The two men heard the EMT woman holler for help as she couldn't control the injured man, even with his dangling arm. An officer ran forward and they soon subdued him long enough for the EMT to stick him with some type of hypodermic needle.

"Well, I guess that answers that question. Someone is in there!"

Right then the observing men heard the siren of the fire engine and a second ambulance approaching in the distance.

CHAPTER THREE

Joshua Warner ached all over and the constant jostling and being poked didn't help. A frown furled his brow as he tried to figure out where he was and why. Slowly, the voices and sounds penetrated his consciousness and memories of metal on metal made Joshua jerk. He tried to rub the grogginess from his eyes, but found himself unable to move. Joshua opened his eyes wide as realization that his whole body was confined hit his brain.

As his mind became more alert, Josh struggled to understand what was happening to him. He felt his body tense and jerk once more.

"Sir, please remain calm. My name is Lynn and I'm an EMT. You've been involved in a bad accident and we're taking you to the hospital."

Josh turned his eyes toward the calm, friendly voice. In spite of her words, something weighed heavy on his mind. . . . Some question he wanted to ask, but couldn't seem to pull up. Instead, he asked with a thick tongue, "Did you give me something to knock me out?"

"Yes, sir. We did. You were uncontrollable and were causing yourself further physical damage." The woman's attention was drawn to the blood pressure cuff inflating on his left arm.

As he waited for her to place a stethoscope to his heart and lungs, Josh took stock of the situation. He couldn't detect any IV drips going, so he surmised his condition must be fairly good. He mentally began running his mind over his body; starting with the feet. All toes moved even under the constraints of the gurney straps. He breathed a sigh of relief and thanked God. As his silent inspection traveled upward, Josh began running into problem areas; particularly with his ribs and right arm.

"Sir, we took the liberty to check your driver's license, so would you please verify for me your name and address?"

Josh's mind was clearing more rapidly now and a sense of urgency hit him as he gave her the information. As he stated his name and address thoughts of Liz surged to the forefront of his mind. "Where's my wife? Where's Lizzie? Is she alright?"

He tried to sit up, but couldn't. A heavy hand landed on his chest as the EMT commanded, "Sir, you must remain calm! If you'll hold still, I'll answer what I can."

Joshua forced himself to do as she said by taking a deep breath which brought on a coughing spasm; which in turn sent an excruciating pain shooting down the right side of his neck, shoulder, and arm. His eyes searched hers for an explanation.

"Mr. Warner, you look to have busted your collar bone and right arm in a few places. That's one of the reasons why you're so securely held to the gurney. I also suspect you have a couple cracked ribs. Most people get those from the seatbelts during an accident."

The woman rattled on about the pros and cons of seatbelts while Joshua fought the pain of his injuries, but more importantly of his heart. The pain had served to wipe away all fuzziness and with it came vivid pictures of the accident and Lizzie pinned in the car.

"Where's Lizzie? Is she. . . .Is she. . . .alive?"

"She was when the ambulance left with her. She's ahead of us. The other EMT's wanted to call the Aero med, but the snow and wind are too heavy." Seeing more questions in his eyes, she hurriedly stated, "Mr. Warner, I really don't know her condition. You were my assignment and my focus. You're both headed to the same hospital. I'm sure someone will fill you in once we arrive and get you both checked over."

The EMT then explained in detail all that needed to be done

once the ambulances arrived at the hospital. In a stern voice, she concluded with, "And Mr. Warner, we'll all be very busy, so give us time to do our jobs and find out what all is wrong and what needs to be done!" In a softer voice she asked, "Okay? Can you do that?"

She watched her patient close his eyes. For a moment she thought he had fallen asleep, but then noticed as tears snuck out to run down the sides of his face. His lips moved, but no sound came out. It was then she realized the man was praying.

Placing her fingers on his pulse, she was amazed to feel his heart rate slow. A few minutes later his eyes opened and a calm assurance flowed from his eyes towards hers. *Why . . . he thinks the prayer helped him!* A momentary sadness hit Lynn as she wished that kind of faith and trust could be for her, too. It was on the tip of her tongue to ask him about his faith. Instead, her professional side said, "So . . . tell me Mr. Warner . . . what do you do for a living?"

Joshua had trouble concentrating, but slowly he replied, "I'm the Pastor of a small country church north of here."

"And how long have you been a Pastor?"

"Let's see . . . a little over six years at this church."

As she continued asking him questions, the EMT took vitals and kept him comfortable. Her thoughts were to test his cognitive abilities, but also to distract her patient from focusing on his wife as the two ambulances hurried toward the hospital.

"So, tell me Reverend, any children, grandchildren?"

CHAPTER FOUR

Sounds of engines, tires on pavement, and even distant sirens filled Elizabeth English with excitement! *I'm so glad I didn't talk myself out of all this!* Liz thought as she gazed in wonder at the activity surrounding her.

While waiting for the first cars to line up at the starting point, Liz's mind drifted back to the day before. It was Saturday and she'd gone to the mall with her cousins. While there, she'd been introduced to a group of four girls her own age. After chatting a bit, one of them invited her to hang out with them the next afternoon. The four girls had giggled and all talked at once!

"It's a blast!"

"All the cool guys come with their muscle cars!"

"We all pitch in with cold soda and snacks."

"And. . . we flirt with the guys!"

Then, like a fine turned quartet, they finished with, "You just have to come with us!"

Once the girls had mentioned "all the cool guys come", Liz's mind was made up. She was open to doing almost anything if it meant possibly seeing Joshua Warner again. So, it was decided the girls would swing by to get her around two, Sunday afternoon.

A short time later the girls turned to leave, when Liz stopped them. "What do I wear?"

One suggested, "Something cool. It will be hot!"

The heavily made-up one said, "Something sexy and tight!"

They all giggled again and turned to leave. Then one stopped. She had been the one to mention earlier about the food and drink. Liz had already zeroed in on her as the practical one and worth knowing better. Now she suggested, "I think sandals, a short sleeved blouse and pedal pushers would do just fine."

Liz nodded and smiled her thanks as the girl left to catch up with her friends. She watched their backs a moment, and then turned to her older cousins. "I think I feel the need to do a little shopping."

The next afternoon, Elizabeth checked herself in the mirror several times before her ride arrived. Feeling confident she looked good, Liz's heart had fluttered as she thought about the possibility of seeing Joshua again. It had been a week since their meeting near the French Quarter and he hadn't called. Elizabeth's romantic heart had envisioned him eagerly calling that very same evening, but she'd hoped in vain. Now, Liz wondered if the whole thing had been some kind of strange dream. Standing in front of the mirror, she stated to her reflection, "What if he does show up and has a girl with him? Have you thought of that? Or, what if he doesn't acknowledge you? Or worse . . . what if he doesn't even remember you?"

Not receiving a reply from the mirrored image, Liz sagged on the edge of the bed. "I can't go today!" She thought irrationally, "If he wanted to talk to me or see me, he'd have called or somehow found me!"

She was at the point of not going when the girls pulled up and blew their horn. Smiling, Elizabeth reconsidered. *Who cares if he shows up or not! This could be fun! Besides there are other guys out there! He's not the only one in the world!*

Having made up her mind, she grabbed a ponytail hold for her long auburn hair and ran down the stairs.

One of her cousins stood by the front door. "Elizabeth, have fun but don't do anything stupid, okay? If for some reason things should get out of hand, you have our number. Call and we'll come get you."

Hugging her close, Liz replied, "Thanks. I'm sure all will be fine."

"I'm not. We keep hearing about drag races going on outside

of town. I hope that's not where these girls are headed."

A short while later, that's exactly where Liz found herself.

Cassie had driven out of town to a straight stretch of road and turned into a now flattened down field of weeds that was rapidly filling with all types and models of cars. Elizabeth wasn't familiar with name brands but some of the cars were extra noisy with big tailpipes and lots of shiny chrome.

Elizabeth felt her heart race with excitement as practical Brandy explained, "This here is usually the starting point. A quarter mile down the road is the home of one of the drivers; which serves as the finish line. Each place has red starter flags and spotters to keep a lookout for oncoming traffic, especially the police. They signal the all clear and the race begins."

By the time she was done explaining, Cassie had opened the door and gotten out. The others quickly followed as Liz asked, "If the finish line is down there, how come we don't go there to see who wins?"

Tight pants Tilly piped up with, "Because this is where the guys all hangout!" She rolled her eyes at Elizabeth as if wondering how anyone could be so dumb; then added, "Besides, the racers come back here to have another go, especially if they keep winning."

"Come on. We usually sit on the front of the car to watch," Brandy said as she hauled out a blanket to spread over the hood.

The three other girls seemed anxious to mingle, so Elizabeth offered to help lay the blanket out. A little while later, Brandy wanted to walk around, too. Sensing Brandy was just staying near to be nice, Elizabeth stated, "I don't know anyone and I really prefer to stay here. So, go with the others. I'll be fine."

Happy to have a moment alone, Liz stood by the car to study her surroundings. Not seeing any sign of Joshua, she experienced a sharp disappointment then wondered if maybe he was at the finish line. Mentally she'd begun practicing various ways to ask the girls if they knew him, when they suddenly ran up all excited.

"Come on, Liz. Let's get situated! The first race is about to start!" Brandy handed her a cold cola, then climbed onto the hood. The others scrambled to follow.

Liz climbed aboard the hood leaned her back against the windshield and was soon drawn into the excitement. Her attention was almost immediately caught by a young man walking to the edge of the road with a red flag on a wooden stick; around his neck hung a pair of binoculars. Two cars pulled up side by side in front of him. Once they were set with their motors revving, he pulled the glasses to his eyes and raised the flag. Now the cars grew louder as they anticipated the flag dropping. Receiving an all clear, down the flag went and with squealing tires the two cars tore off!

Over the next hour or so, Elizabeth watched cars pair off and race time and time again. She'd never been involved with anything so exciting! For the first half hour or so, she occasionally scanned the crowds for Joshua, but eventually became so engrossed in the excitement happening around her that she'd forgotten all about him.

One time she ventured to ask, "Is this illegal? Do the police ever come?"

Tilly, the tight shirt and pants girl, popped her gum before replying, "It may be illegal, but the police don't bother us. I think it's because we never have fights or drinking here. It's like an unwritten rule among us. As long as we keep it that way, the police will leave us alone."

"Besides, we've never had any accidents, either," one of the other girls supplied.

To which Brandy responded, "They've come close a couple times, though."

"Yeah! Remember that stranger who came once? We all thought he looked too young to be driving . . . let alone racing! Anyway, when he popped his foot off the brake, his car swerved toward the other one. It was real close!"

So, the afternoon wore on and grew hotter. As the races continued one car in particular began to stand out. It was a 1964 midnight blue GTO. After its third win, Liz asked about it.

"Oh, that's Eddie. His GTO is fast, and I might add, so is he!" Tilly responded enthusiastically. Liz could tell by the tone she used, that he was just Tilly's kind of guy.

Focusing on the car, Liz said, "That's a Goat? I always wondered what one looked like!"

"A goat? You called it a goat?" Tilly asked incredulously.

"Sure. That's what we call GTO's in Michigan."

The girls all laughed, and then Tilly said, "I wouldn't say that in front of fast Eddie. He takes great pride in his car. He might think calling it a goat is an insult." She then added, "That's no way to refer to a car that's never been beat."

The girls grew silent then Brandy said, "He was once, remember?"

Frowning, Tilly raised her chin and stated, "That wasn't a fair race. He had an unfair head start on Eddie."

Liz listened with interest as her words drew comments from the other three girls.

"He did not!"

"That race was fair! Everyone says so!"

"You just love Eddie so are standing up for him!"

Tilly leveled her eyes at the last comment before shrugging her shoulders to say, "Yah, well, it doesn't matter now does it? He doesn't come here to race anymore, so Eddie can still strut around as King!"

"That's exactly what he thinks about himself!" Brandy muttered next to Liz's ear.

Liz turned to study Brandy's face. With raised eyebrows,

she decided Brandy didn't have much use for fast Eddie. "Which one is Eddie?" she asked.

Tilly primped herself and sat a little straighter as she replied, "The handsome one walking this way."

Liz turned to watch a medium sized guy with a cigarette pack stuck in his rolled up shirt sleeve headed straight for them. His hair was slicked back and the top shirt buttons were undone revealing the beginnings of a hairy chest.

Not wanting him to catch her staring, Liz turned her eyes toward the next two cars lined up to race.

A few seconds later, she heard, "Well, hi there, girls. Who's the redhead?"

Ever since elementary school, whenever she'd been teased about her red hair and freckles, Elizabeth had developed a strong dislike to anyone making references to her hair color. There were times she'd even come to blows over the issue. As she grew older, her hair and freckles had ceased to be made fun of. But now, those old familiar feelings of rage surfaced and Liz felt her body stiffen and hands clench. Choosing to ignore him, she concentrated on the two cars squealing off the line.

"Hey, Red! I've not seen you here before. What's your name?"

Liz fought to maintain control of her temper.

Finding imaginary lint on her shorts, she flicked it off while

Brandy stated angrily, "Her name isn't Red! It's Elizabeth!"

Turning thankful eyes her way, Elizabeth smiled then slowly directed her eyes at the offending young man.

Undaunted, Eddie stepped closer. "Well, hello there . . . E-liz-a-beth, or shall I call you, Lizzie?"

Elizabeth pasted a tight smile on her face. "Actually, I prefer Liz or Elizabeth."

Shrugging, he said, "Either way, doll. My name is Eddie and I was wondering if you'd like to ride with me in my next race?"

By the way a couple of her friends gasped, Liz surmised the offer was a rare one. Venturing a glance at Tilly, Liz was startled to see anger verging on hatred directed her way. The last thing Elizabeth intended was getting into a car with this guy, let alone creating a problem with her newfound friend. Bothered with the situation he was trying to put her in, Elizabeth's dislike of the guy grew. She wanted to tell him to get lost, but had been taught not to be rude, so said the first excuse that came to her mind. "I'm sorry...Eddie. I'm waiting for someone. We were supposed to meet here."

At her words, Elizabeth felt the eyes of her companions all swing her way. She knew her supposed date was news to them and hoped none of them would question her about it.

But, she didn't have to worry, for Eddie didn't give them a chance. "Well, since he isn't here yet, where's the harm? Who is this guy anyway?"

"That would be me," a voice confidently stated from off to her right.

Elizabeth's heart skipped several beats at the sound of Joshua Warner's voice, then caught rapidly back up. She turned a genuine smile his way.

Eddie and her friends had also turned.

"Well, Joshua Warner. How are you? I haven't seen you around here for a long time."

Out of the corner of her eye, Elizabeth studied Eddie's face. His words had the form of being friendly, but they'd come out hard and his eyes had narrowed.

"It hasn't worked out for me to come," Josh casually replied before turning his focus back to Liz.

But, Eddie wasn't done. "Did you bring your Chevelle?"

Joshua's mannerism revealed he'd seen this coming. Turning back to Eddie, he replied, "I sure did. It seemed like a beautiful day for racing."

As the two guys talked, all Liz wanted to do was keep her eyes on Joshua's face. He appeared so calm and at ease; which was in sharp contrast to Eddie's tight face and frowning brow. It was obvious he didn't like Joshua, but as yet, Liz hadn't discovered why. Swinging her attention to the friends sitting next to her on the hood, she was further intrigued to find their eyes darting back and forth between Eddie and Joshua. Suddenly, the earlier talk about someone beating Eddie came filtering into her mind and Liz turned startled eyes Josh's direction. *Had it been him? Had Joshua's Chevelle beaten Eddie's GTO?*

She had become so absorbed in the thought, that Elizabeth almost missed Joshua's next words, "Liz, I'm sorry to be so late." Extending his hand, he then asked, "Will you walk with me a moment? I'd like to show you my car."

Liz took his hand while stuttering, "S-s-sure."

Once off the hood, she let his hand go to straighten the legs of her shorts.

Eddie stepped closer. Ignoring Joshua, he asked again, "So, Lizzie, would you like to ride with me in my next race?"

She stiffened at his easy use of "Lizzie", and then did something totally out of character. Stepping closer to Joshua, she laced her arm around his elbow while saying, "Sorry, Eddie. If I ride with anyone it will be with Josh."

Now, it was Joshua's turn to stiffen. It was far too late to take back her words as Liz realized how much of a challenge that sounded.

"Fine! Let's do it, Joshua. You and me – right now!"

Joshua hesitated while looking down into Elizabeth's fearful, yet apologetic eyes.

He smiled warmly, which sent tingles right down to her toes.

Joshua seemed to understand that she'd never been inside a racing car before and his eyes revealed that to her. In spite of her fluttering heart at the look in his eyes, Elizabeth felt herself calming. She suddenly felt a need to let him know she'd stick by whatever he decided to do . . . whether to race or not. Lifting her chin, Elizabeth gave Joshua a slight nod.

Never taking his warm hazel eyes from her vivid blue ones, Joshua stated to the hovering Eddie, "Okay. But give me a few minutes to talk Liz through the process. I don't think she's ever done this before." He then placed his hand over hers still in the crook of his arm and turned her toward his vehicle.

Once out of earshot, Elizabeth whispered, "Thanks for playing along and rescuing me. I'm so sorry for putting you in this situation! Why don't we just get in the car and leave?" Startled at her last words, Liz stopped walking causing Joshua to halt his forward progress; a look of embarrassment at her own boldness filled her face.

Joshua studied Elizabeth's reddening face, and then chuckled. "You're fine, Liz. I came here looking for you."

"You did? For me? How'd you know I'd be here?" Elizabeth felt like she was babbling like a silly girl, but couldn't seem to help it. His words had taken her completely by surprise.

Still smiling warmly, Joshua said, "It was such a beautiful afternoon, I felt like getting the Chevelle on the road. I called the number on the napkin. Your cousin said you were out with four new friends. I figured your friends would bring you here."

He started her moving again and was soon guiding her around a fire engine red 1965 Chevelle SS 396. He proudly explained that she had 9-inch slicks and headers.

Most of his words didn't mean a thing to Liz, but she didn't care. It was nice hearing his voice again and savoring the fact that he'd actually come there looking for her.

Once Joshua had proudly presented his baby, he then explained about the race; and what Elizabeth could expect. As he finished an idea occurred. "Win or lose, I like the idea you had about us leaving. How about you telling your friends we're going for ice cream or something and that I'll see that you get home?"

Not wasting time in case he changed his mind, Liz ran to briefly explain the plan. The girls were full of questions, but she didn't have time to explain. Apologizing, Elizabeth thanked the girls for bringing her, and then ran back to Joshua. In short order, she found herself strapped into the revving Chevelle on the start line with the noisy GTO immediately to their right. Leaning forward, Elizabeth glanced at Eddie. His jaw was set as he stared forward.

The red flag went up and Liz's heart raced as she tensely pushed herself back into the seat. *What am I doing? I could get killed!* Fear coursed through her veins as Liz clasped her hands tightly together. For the first time, the thought of praying came to mind, which was startling to Elizabeth. Chuckling nervously, Liz said under her breath, "I'm not even sure I believe in God."

Right then, the flag dropped and the Chevelle shot forward throwing Liz further into the seat. For a few seconds the cars were neck and neck, and then Joshua surged forward - crossing the finish line first.

At the drop of the flag, Elizabeth realized she'd been holding her breath. Now, she exhaled and then rapidly sucked in fresh air. She'd never experienced such an exciting thing before and Elizabeth felt exhilarated and proud! Her mind started shouting – *We won! We really won! My man won! My man won!* As her mind caught up with the phrases roaring around in her head, the words - *My man* – claimed Elizabeth's attention as Joshua proudly announced, "We did it, Lizzie! We won!"

Still moving down the road, Joshua slowed the car to the appropriate speed as they headed toward town.

Elizabeth looked with admiration at Joshua's driving skills and happy face. All the while marveling at how much nicer "Lizzie" sounded on Joshua's lips . . . compared to the offensive Eddie's.

As the car neared town, Elizabeth stared out her side window and briefly closed her eyes. *I can't believe Joshua came and that I'm here with him now.*

Suddenly the car stopped moving. Elizabeth's eyes sprung open as she swung her eyes toward Joshua. But he wasn't there.

No one was there.

Elizabeth frowned as she tried remembering the sound of the car door opening and closing, but didn't. Frantically she checked the back seat and then out all the windows.

Joshua wasn't there. He wasn't anywhere. He'd vanished in thin air!

Elizabeth's heart raced as she moved to open the car door, but instead found herself in front of a wooden door with a large knocker. Figuring Joshua may already be on the other side, a thoroughly confused Elizabeth grabbed hold and rapped it several times on the massive door. When it swung open, Elizabeth saw nothing but – white emptiness.

And . . . Joshua was nowhere to be found.

CHAPTER FIVE

"Mr. Warner, I have a cell phone. Is there anyone you'd like me to call before we arrive at the hospital?"

Joshua Warner focused on the kindly EMT, and then said hesitantly with heavy sighs, "Yes. Could you please call my eldest son? His number is in my wallet."

Closing his eyes tightly, he suddenly groaned, "Oh, Lizzie!"

A chocking sob escaped with his last words, and then to Joshua's embarrassment, a well of tears broke loose.

Putting a warm hand on his good arm, the EMT softly said, "Mr. Warner, it will be okay. You'll see."

When Joshua's ambulance arrived at the hospital and his gurney was removed, he noticed lots of activity at a booth to his left.

Catching his breath, he had only a moment to wonder if it was his Lizzie before he was moved to his own cubicle. Over the next couple hours, many tests were done. Joshua was informed that his collarbone was indeed fractured; his right arm was broken in two places below the elbow, and that two of his fingers on the right hand were broken.

Once the x-rays were shown to Joshua the doctor stated an operating room would be prepared, then explained what the surgeon would be doing with the fractures. "You're lucky that's all the damage done. I fully expected internal injuries, but found only bruising, which included the ribs."

He paused to check his chart, so Joshua took that moment to calmly state, "Luck didn't have anything to do with it."

The doctor looked up. "What did you just say?"

"I don't believe in luck, Doc. My life is in the hands of my heavenly Father. Whatever happens is according to His will. Luck has nothing to do with it," he re-stated firmly with conviction.

Not making any comment, the doctor studied Joshua's face, then mumbled something under his breath as he turned back to the chart.

Joshua let the silence linger a few minutes before asking, "Doctor, is there any word on my wife, Elizabeth Warner? One nurse told me she was being prepped for surgery and that she was in critical condition." Reaching with his good hand, he placed it on the doctor's arm. "Please, doc. Before I go to surgery would you please find out what you can?"

The doctor stared at the chart as if not hearing, then flipped it closed. For the first time, Joshua detected some compassion on his face. He assured in a hurried voice, "I'll find out what I can," before turning away to leave. At the door, he said over his shoulder, "The anesthesiologist will be in to see you shortly."

"Thank you, doctor. Thank you very much."

CHAPTER SIX

"Hi. Have you been here long?"

A couple days earlier, a friend of Tilly's had decided a barn dance would be a perfect birthday gift to himself, so hired a live band and spread the word. Thinking Joshua Warner would probably show up, Liz had willingly agreed to accompany her friends. Upon walking in, she'd scanned the room for his presence but was disappointed to not see him anywhere. After an hour had gone by and he still hadn't made an appearance, Elizabeth seriously contemplated go home, when his words sounded close to her ear.

Elizabeth stopped swaying to the live band music as her heart skipped a few beats. She fought to steady it while slowly turning to reply, "I've been here an hour or so."

She tried to sound casual and uncaring while lowering her eyes to smooth her full skirt. But, her indifference fled when Elizabeth brought her eyes back to his handsome face. He smiled warmly into her eyes, and then introduced her to a friend standing close by. "This is Ben." He then asked Liz what she was drinking and if she'd like to join them for a beer. Not a beer drinker, Elizabeth declined, but said a cold soda sounded great. Joshua gave Ben a nod, who promptly left to get the drinks.

As Ben walked off, Elizabeth watched Joshua scan the crowd then turn his attention back to her. "Did you come alone?"

"No, I came with Tilly, Cassie, Brandy, and Mel." Looking around she added, "They're here somewhere. They've been dancing."

"What about you? Have you been dancing, or don't you dance?"

Blushing, Elizabeth didn't want to tell him she'd already turned down five guys while waiting for his appearance.

The most insistent had been Eddie.

Instead, she opted to say, "No dancing so far. I've been wandering around getting the lay of the land, so to speak. I'd just wound up here, when you walked up."

As she spoke her eyes roamed the room and widened at the amount of people. Two thirds of the huge barn was made up of tables and chairs, leaving space up front for dancing. At the very front was a large raised platform which housed the band. Being so focused on searching for Joshua, Liz hadn't paid attention until that moment that the barn was getting full.

Placing a hand on her elbow, he stated, "We'd better get a seat before they're all gone." He then steered her toward the front tables closest to the dance area. Liz was surprised to see little placards on the table saying – reserved. She started to comment on that when the host walked up slapping Joshua on the shoulder. "Glad you could make it buddy! As you can see, I saved the best tables for you and your friends. Enjoy yourselves." He stayed long enough to receive Joshua's birthday wishes, and then moved on to another group of people.

Impressed, Elizabeth quietly took the seat Joshua pulled out for her. Like magnets, Liz's friends began appearing to claim some of the seats. Liz started to stop them when Joshua assured her the seats were for Elizabeth and her friends. Two tables were put end to end and began rapidly filling. All Liz' friends plus several of Josh's were now seated, except for Tilly. She was nowhere to be seen.

As the crowd grew noisy in chatter, Ben walked up with arms full of cold drinks. "I saw the girls arrive so doubled back for more. I hope cola and root beer are good enough for those who don't drink beer. That's all I grabbed." With that, he handed Joshua a cold beer, then set the rest of the drinks on the table to a murmur of

"Thanks", "I'm famished", and "This will hit the spot."

Joshua had seated Elizabeth in the chair closest to the wall facing the band and sat down beside her. Ben sat next to Josh and soon struck up a conversation with Brandy seated across from him. As the crowd grew louder, the band became more intent on their playing. The music was loud so in order to talk Liz and Joshua had to lean toward each other. A couple times, Joshua's leg brushed her thigh and goose bumps raced up Liz's spine into her heart. She wondered if he was experiencing the same effect, but didn't say anything.

To Elizabeth's consternation, periodically their talking was interrupted by girls wanting to dance with Joshua and Ben. A couple times Ben left, but Joshua always declined. It puzzled Liz that so many asked, because Josh didn't seem to be the dancing type; which disappointed Elizabeth, for she loved to dance and had been impatiently waiting for him to arrive so she could. Now it appeared he didn't like to and since he'd arrived, no other guys had come to ask her. Hiding her frustration, Elizabeth decided to be content just sitting near him, but as the music played she couldn't help humming along and tapping her toes in tune with the beat.

After about an hour of playing, the band took a break and their host took the microphone. "Hello, everyone!"

A chorus of voices hollered back greetings as Elizabeth leaned in to whisper in Joshua's ear, "What's he doing?"

When Joshua turned to respond, his face was within inches of hers. For a few seconds they were lost in each other's eyes, before he softly replied, "I don't know."

Nervous at his continued nearness, Liz broke eye contact and pulled back as the host explained, "Since the band is taking a break, we're going to use the turntable, so don't think the dancing has stopped. I want to thank you all for coming. Have fun but remember – Don't drink and drive! You're welcome to drink, but make sure you ride home with someone who hasn't. I don't want any accidents on my birthday!" As he spoke, periodically people would raise glasses and holler out – Happy Birthday! The host finished his little speech to seriously scan the crowd and then he jumped into a whole different frame of mind. Yelling into the mike he asked, "So, are you ready for some more dancing?"

Several yelled – "YES"!

"I said, are you ready for some dancing?"

That time, to Liz's ears it sounded like the whole room responded with a resounding yes.

"Then get ready for some . . . WIPEOUT!"

With that, he signaled the music to start and left the stage.

To Elizabeth's surprise, Joshua stood to her right. Leaning close to her ear, he asked, "Shall we?" and then extended his hand.

Liz was momentarily shocked. Of all songs to dance to this was one of the fastest! She raised questioning eyebrows Joshua's way thinking he was teasing, but the hand remained extended.

"Well? Are you game, or not?"

That decided it! Taking a firm hold of his hand, Liz came to her feet. "I'm game if you are!"

Smiling deeply, he replied, "That's my girl," then lead her to the rapidly filling dance floor.

Elizabeth had a passion for dancing and wondered how he would do, but soon lost her worries. His body moved very well to the music and Liz was delighted. Now she understood why so many girls had asked him to dance. His body was one well put together human machine of beat and rhythm! Losing all sense of shyness, the two moved to the fast music.

As the music drew to a close, many left the floor, but several stayed as the DJ put on another song. This was a song Elizabeth loved singing along with, so she did. "My love is brighter than the brightest star that shines every night above." Elizabeth had no idea how much personality she was demonstrating as she sang and danced. If she'd looked closer to Joshua's face, she'd have seen a possessive glint in his eyes. For the first time Joshua was getting a glimpse of the totally relaxed Elizabeth and he liked what he was seeing.

Once that song drew to a close, Liz was hot and ready to sit down. Joshua seemed to be of the same mind until a slow dance started. Within seconds, Elizabeth found herself expertly swung back onto the dance floor. When Josh's hand touched her waist and he captured her other one, she grew warm all over. As they moved to the music his hands tightened and their bodies inched closer. He soon had her hand snuggled between them close to his heart.

For a few moments, they were the only two people in the room, that is . . . until a voice broke the cloud they were enveloped in.

"Well, isn't that sweet. Hey, Red, how about dancing with me? Get lost Josh, I'm cutting in."

By the way Eddie slurred his words; it was obvious he'd been drinking long before coming to the dance.

Elizabeth stiffened as Joshua ordered in her ear, "Stay behind me!" as he smoothly moved her in back. Then letting out a heavy sigh he faced Eddie.

Liz leaned slightly to the left in order to see Eddie as he swayed with Tilly glued to his arm. Elizabeth was shocked at the open anger blazing from Tilly's eyes towards her. Frowning, Elizabeth looked with concern at Eddie. She wondered why he wanted a dance with her with Tilly on his arm. By the look of Tilly, it didn't seem to be setting well with her either. Liz mulled over the whole situation as Joshua stepped closer to Eddie.

"Hey, Eddie, ease up buddy. We're all here to have a good time celebrating a birthday."

Eddie roughly pushed Tilly aside while take a menacing step

toward Joshua. "Exactly! The good time I plan to have is me and Red getting to know each other better!"

He moved to step around Joshua, but found his way hindered when Josh sidestepped into his path. With a strong, yet strangely quiet voice, he said, "Turn around, Eddie. She's with me and doesn't want to dance with you. You need to seriously think about what you're doing! You really don't want to make an issue of this!"

Eddie let out an ugly sneer while stating, "Yes, yes I do!" and lunged at Joshua with his fist raised.

Elizabeth stiffened and took a step back as she waited to hear the punch connect, but it never did. Joshua easily knocked it away with one hand while using the other to wave Elizabeth to back up further. It amazed her that he seemed fully aware of everything going on around him, even her whereabouts. Obeying, Liz took a few steps backward, and then felt someone tugging her arm. It was Brandy. "Stand over here, Elizabeth. This could get ugly fast!" As she spoke, Brandy pulled her to a safe distance away.

Elizabeth now had a much better view of the situation as Ben and a couple other friends moved closer to the two men. It alarmed her to see Eddie's friends do the same. The scene didn't look good as Eddie took another swing at Joshua.

Having nursed only one beer over the last couple hours, Joshua's senses were sharp and controlled. In spite of Eddie's repeated attempts to hit him, Josh easily fended him off; yet never made a threat of retaliation, which strangely fueled Eddie's rage.

As more and more people drew around the men, one of Eddie's buddies stated he was ready to help which prompted Ben to calmly step toward the new voice. Elizabeth could see that everyone was tense; ready for a fight. Yet, everyone held their places as Eddie seemed to pause. Liz thought he looked to quit, when suddenly, Tilly handed Eddie an empty beer bottle then backed away. The bottle in his hand seemed to transform Eddie before everyone's eyes. Tilly's action turned him into a raging bull as he charged forward while swinging the bottle.

Elizabeth saw Joshua's body tense and his fist raise as Eddie came close. He dodged a couple wild swings of the bottle, then quick as a whip, Josh's fist came forward connecting with Eddie's chin and he crumbled like a rag doll.

That was all his buddies needed. Screaming profanities, the fight was on. Like a chain reaction more and more guys became involved and fists were flying all over the room. Soon chairs were being tossed and bottles thrown.

Elizabeth became increasingly upset and lost track of Joshua in the fray. She was thankful Brandy, Cassie, and Melody were standing near. It was all they could do to stay out of the path of flying objects. By the time a flying bottle tore a hole in the front of the bass drum, Liz was close to falling apart when Joshua and their host suddenly appeared in front of the frightened girls.

Joshua put his comforting arm around Elizabeth's shoulder. She turned her head into his chest as the host said, "This is out of hand and the police have been called. It's best you all leave now. There's a side door toward the back of the bandstand."

Joshua briefly squeezed Elizabeth then released her to firmly take hold of her hand. Turning to her friends, he said, "It's time to go, girls. Follow close behind Liz and me." Using his body as a shield to protect them from flying objects, Joshua maneuvered guys aside as he led the girls across the dance floor to the opposite side of the room. Opening the back door, Joshua motioned the girls out, when Elizabeth paused.

"Joshua, I came with Tilly. We must find her."

For the first time, Elizabeth saw anger cross Josh's face. "You've got to be kidding, Liz!"

"Please, Joshua?"

Exasperated, Joshua stared perplexed at Elizabeth. "Liz, are you forgetting who gave Eddie the beer bottle? Much of what's happening now is Tilly's fault! Why should you care about her?"

"She made a bad mistake, but she's still my friend," Liz replied in a pleading voice while scanning the room.

He stared at her a second, then said in a calmer voice, "Lizzie, she could be anywhere. We need to leave now."

At that moment, Brandy piped up with, "Over there! See her? She's huddled under that table."

Quickly assessing the situation, Joshua made a decision. Turning to Ben who'd been following protectively near, he asked, "Ben, will you take the girls out while I get Tilly?"

As he spoke sirens were clearly heard pulling up to the front of the barn.

"Let's hurry girls," Ben urged as Joshua turned to go rescue Tilly.

Being first through the door, Elizabeth found herself in a dark room. Momentarily confused, she froze.

"Let's see if there's a light switch around here." Ben said.

Within seconds he had the area illuminated and Elizabeth found herself in a small attached tool shed.

She paused in bewilderment as to her next move when Ben urged, "Keep moving forward, Elizabeth."

Behind them they could hear police whistles and a bullhorn commanding everyone to stand still.

Now that Liz could see her surroundings, she saw another door just a short distance away. Taking a step back, she instructed the other girls to go ahead. Her plan was to wait for Joshua and Tilly, but by the time the other girls got out the new door Joshua and Tilly were by Liz's side.

Tilly was weeping hysterically and Liz noted Joshua had his arm around her shoulder. For a fleeting second, Elizabeth felt a surge of jealousy, but then realized he was partly doing it to steady the wobbly Tilly, but also to keep her moving forward.

Noting the momentary look on Elizabeth's face, Joshua motioned for Ben to take Tilly then reached for Elizabeth's hand.

In a few more seconds all of them were outside in the fresh air.

Elizabeth inhaled deeply as Ben asked, "Tilly, where are you parked?"

"Out front," she managed between gasping sobs.

Joshua emitted a frustrated grunt as he instructed Ben and the girls to keep moving toward the parked cars. Several cars were already leaving, but more police were arriving.

"Where, Tilly? Where's your car?" Ben questioned.

Brandy supplied, "It's over there by the big oak tree."

Relieved it was close; Joshua pulled Elizabeth to a stop. "Do any of you girls have a driver's license?"

"I do," Cassie stated.

"Actually, we all do," Brandy informed to anyone interested.

"Okay then. Tilly isn't up to driving, so I think it would be best if one of you did it for her."

Cassie volunteered.

Liz moved to follow the girls, but Joshua held her still. Projecting his voice forward to the group already moving to Tilly's car, he stated, "Elizabeth will be with me. I'll see she gets home."

Liz raised eyebrows at his statement but didn't resist.

Joshua walked her to his large Dodge truck. Taking her to the passenger side, he opened the door then went to assist her up into the cab, but stopped when he noted the look on her face. Leaning closer he asked, "Are you alright?"

To Liz's consternation, her body began to shake and a lump formed in her throat. Unable to speak, she turned tear brimmed eyes up to his and shook her head in the negative. Within seconds she found herself wrapped in his warm comforting arms. As tears freely flowed she tried to explain that she'd never experienced anything like that before.

"Oh-h, Lizzie. I'm sorry you went through that. Everything's all right now."

He kissed the top of her head, and then pulled back slightly with his arms still around her. With a teasing voice, he said, "It's your entire fault, you know."

At his words, Elizabeth stiffened. Her head flew off his shoulder as she tried pulling away, but was held fast.

Joshua's eyes roamed her hair then landed on her red eyes and nose. He pulled a folded hanky from his back pocket to gently wipe her eyes and cheeks. He then added softly, "If you weren't so darn cute with your red hair, blue eyes and freckles, we wouldn't be in this mess in the first place."

As he held Elizabeth's gaze, she forgot all about the fight, the police, and the loud sounds around her . . . everything. All she could think of were his warm hazel eyes, which were growing darker by the second, and his handsome face. As his gaze lowered to her lips, Elizabeth kept thinking, *He's going to kiss me. He's going to kiss me.*

Sure enough, he slowly leaned in and Elizabeth closed her eyes in anticipation.

Then . . . she felt a soft kiss on her forehead.

When her eyes sprang open, he cocked his head and then planted one on the end of her nose before whispering, "All better now?"

Unable to utter a word, Elizabeth resorted to nodding her head in the affirmative.

Taking a deep breath and exhaling, Joshua smiled broadly and stepped back. "Good, then up you go."

He placed his hands on her waist and lifted her into the cab. He then leaned in to make sure her seatbelt was securely fastened. With his face hovering near hers, he asked, "All cozy?"

Elizabeth finally found her voice to reply a little too breathlessly, "Yes, yes, I'm fine thank you."

"Good." He smiled deeply once more then backed out to shut the door.

Yes, I'm fine thank you!! What a moron I am! Here's a handsome, wonderful guy trying to make me feel special and that's the best I can do?

Liz inhaled and exhaled heavily as Joshua opened the driver side door and got in. As he inserted the key, she noticed the knuckles of his right hand. "Joshua, you're bleeding!"

He lifted his hand from the keys to briefly survey the damage, and then shrugged. "It's nothing. Besides, it's a small price to pay for protecting, my Lizzie."

His smile and words carried Elizabeth's heart repeatedly to her toes and back.

As they drove away her mind and heart kept saying, *My Lizzie. He called me – My Lizzie.*

A warm feeling coursed through Liz's veins as the words played over and over in her mind, prompting her to explain to Joshua how she was affected by them. But as she turned to express herself Elizabeth found she was once more in the white room.

Joshua and his truck had disappeared.

Confusion and anxiety threatened to consume her as Elizabeth realized she'd lost him - - again!

CHAPTER SEVEN

Joshua underwent surgery and now lay in a hospital bed with his arm all bandaged and propped on a pillow. The surgeon had to do some reconstruction with pins and plates, so opted to tape up the collarbone until surgery at a later date. Joshua felt quite trussed up and dopey from drugs, but as soon as they brought him from recovery he began asking about Elizabeth. He was impatient for news and grew irate to the point the nurse threatened to sedate him if he didn't calm down. Wanting to make himself perfectly clear on the subject, Joshua threw the covers off with his left hand preparing to rise when the doctor walked in, demanding, "Just what do you think you're doing?"

"Doc, I need to know about my wife! It's been hours and

I've not heard a word."

To which the doctor promptly responded that he'd find out what he could under the condition that Joshua be a good patient and stay in bed. He then checked the arm bandages, gave the nurse a couple instructions and exited the room. The nurse talked under her breath about Joshua's recent action as she examined his IV site making sure it was still functioning well.

Ignoring her, Joshua impatiently watched the door until the doctor re-entered a short time later.

Without any preamble, he announced, "Mr. Warner, I have to tell you . . . your wife's prognosis isn't good."

A feeling of despair threatened to consume Joshua as he fought through the lingering drugs to understand the doctor's next words.

"The surgeon will be in later to speak extensively with you but for now he said I could report that she's quite busted up on her right side; two broken ribs, a fractured hipbone and multiple breaks on her leg and arm. At this time, nothing will be done for the ribs and hipbone. They spent hours repairing her leg and arm and the operating surgeon reports that those surgeries went very well. Your wife's bone density is good, which was a positive with so much work having to be done. Like you, she has plates and pins. Her right leg and arm are in large casts."

Here the doctor paused. When Joshua didn't respond, the

doctor saw he was still struggling to absorb all he was saying. He studied him a moment then said more slowly, "Mr. Warner, she also has some abdominal edema."

"What's . . . what's that mean?"

"It means she's got some fluid built up in the abdomen. Scans show she received lacerations to her liver and spleen. They are most likely the reason for the build-up. They've drawn off a pint of fluid and are monitoring it closely."

He paused a moment and then added, "The amazing thing is that her vital signs are good. They are maintaining good levels, but that could change in seconds."

His agony must have shown on his face, for the doctor said, "Mr. Warner . . . may I call you Joshua?"

Joshua nodded his head while saying in a low, tired voice, "Of course."

"Well, Joshua, I hope it's a comfort to know that she's heavily sedated so as not to feel anything, but . . . you need to know that she took quite a beating and the next 24 hours are critical."

He let that sink in and then quietly added, "I'm sorry, Joshua. The doctors are doing what they can."

Joshua waited for him to say more, but instead he saw a frown cross the doctor's face followed by a look of uncertainty. Keeping his eyes on the docs face, he wondered about the uncertainty when the doctor stood straighter and said, "You mentioned earlier about being a praying man. If that's true, now would be the best time to start talking to your God."

Obviously uncomfortable over the words he had just spoken, the doctor turned to leave.

As he reached the door, Joshua found his voice. "Is there any way I can see her?" His voice broke as he pleaded, "Doc, I need to see her and touch her hand."

Giving Joshua a sad shake of his head he said, "That's not possible. I've already stated that she's heavily sedated, plus she's still in recovery." He turned to leave, but stopped. Joshua watched him stare at the floor a long while before saying, "Tell you what. When the nurse gets you up later, we'll see where your wife's at and about possibly wheeling you down to see her." He then turned to state very clearly, "This is a – we'll see – not a promise; and, I'm not sure you'll get close enough to touch her."

Not realizing he'd been holding his breath, Joshua let it out with a loud rush as he exclaimed fervently, "Thanks, doctor. Thank you very much."

As the doctor left and the door closed, an overwhelming despair started covering Joshua's heart and soul. A few seconds later, as he continued staring into the ever darkening space between him and his Lizzie, Josh heard the nurse softly walk out too.

As soon as the door closed for the second time, Joshua's sobs tore themselves out of his heaving chest, threatening to choke him.

A long while later, the sobs turned into a fervent, pleading prayer to His Heavenly Father on behalf of his beloved Lizzie.

~ ~ ~ ~ ~ ~ ~ ~ ~ ~

Over two hours had gone by and Joshua still hadn't seen Elizabeth. His body had overruled his desires to see her as soon as possible, for he fell into a deep sleep lasting until the nurse woke him for vitals. When he questioned the nurse about his wife, Joshua was pleased to hear that she had been moved to a room in CCU.

"And, Mr. Warner, I explained the situation to her assigned nurse and asked if you could come up. She told me once they finish getting her settled . . . and . . . **if** . . . she's showing stable signs, then they'll see about getting you in there."

Seeing his eyebrows furrow, she fluffed his pillow while clucking, "Now, now, Mr. Warner. That's better than their saying no isn't it?"

"Yes, you're right. Thank you for finding out for me."

He asked her to put the head of his bed up some, she then readjusted all the pillows while saying, and "You were sleeping so soundly, I went ahead and disconnected your phone. The nurse's station has been receiving calls from your children, so when you're up to it; I'll help you call them."

In that moment, Joshua revamped his first impressions of the nurse when she had seemed indifferent to his need for news of Elizabeth. Now, she was going above and beyond, which he greatly appreciated.

"Thank you for all your help. I'm wondering, before I start calling my children, could I have a cup of coffee with cream?"

"Sure thing; regular or decaf?"

"Let's make it regular. I want to be good and awake when we go see my sweetheart."

The nurse smiled broadly as she left to do his bidding.

A while later, having been refreshed with a steaming cup of coffee, Joshua picked up the phone. It was time to update his kids. Before punching in the local number to their eldest son, Joshua paused as pictures of his three children growing up flooded his mind. They'd been a close family. True . . . while they were growing up, Elizabeth was the one they came to first with details of their days, hurtful words from friends, or fun moments. But as they grew into the teen years, the three had begun turning more to Joshua with the more difficult things; confusion about God or the Bible and how those two things related to their lives. Another thing he and Liz had promoted was an open door to any friends the kids wanted to bring home; which many times included needy ones from split homes or ones struggling with the world's tugs on them. Liz always made sure the frig and cupboards had ample snacks readily available.

Now their three kids were out of the home and in their late twenties, early thirties. Their eldest, thirty-two year old Anthony (or Tony as he preferred to be called) was as steady and level headed as a rock. It had taken him until his eleventh year of age before he decided living for Jesus was the life for him. Joshua's mind reminisced how Tony knelt in the living room to pray for Christ to come into His life. After that, Joshua was sure his son would go into the pastorate, but Tony's heart leaned toward the world of computers. So off he went to get his computer science degree at Michigan State. But, in his second year, his direction changed as Tony became more and more involved with one of the campus ministries. His junior year he had switched majors and had gone into the Social Sciences field. Upon graduating, he began looking for a position dealing with troubled teens and was hired in the Detroit area.

But, a year ago his life had taken another direction again. Reflecting back, neither Joshua nor Elizabeth were surprised when Tony announced his desire to quit the high paying, social worker job and took a position as Youth Pastor at a large church in Grand Rapids, Michigan. From the start, it was obvious that God's hand was on Tony's decision, for Tony's youth group had almost doubled since he'd taken it over. An added bonus was Tony meeting a lovely girl who attended the same church. The two of them had been dating for some time.

Just that morning he and Liz had been speculating about an engagement between those two in the near future. Images of Liz's excited face at the prospect sent Joshua's thoughts plummeting.

Forcing his mind away from that train of thought, Joshua's jumped over their next born to zero in on their youngest, Seth. His brows knit into a frown as he thought about the distance that had come between them over the last couple years. Seth was the one who even at a young age had questioned everything concerning Jesus and the relevance of the Bible in today's world. Believing in Christ and asking him into your heart seemed too old school in Seth's mind. He seemed to thrive better with good works and to that end he'd gone overboard. Not strong in the academics, Seth had chosen to join the work force upon graduation from high school. Not long after, he'd found a buddy at work and the two of them shared an apartment. This buddy was affiliated with a heavy works religion which fit right in with Seth's thinking about Christianity, so he plunged in head first. A couple years later, he wound up spent and burned out on the whole Christianity thing. Now, at the age of twenty-six, Seth had recently announced to his parents that he'd come to the conclusion that Jesus existed, but was in fact, just a good man – not the Son of God. It broke Joshua's and Liz's hearts to hear him. Now a fear came in that the accident could be the perfect excuse for Seth to reason that if Jesus truly was God's Son, He never would have allowed the accident to happen in the first place.

Not liking where his thoughts were heading again, Joshua thought on their middle child and only daughter, twenty-eight year old Jennifer. Jenny was a strong willed, independent, yet

70

compassionate woman. She's the one who mainly brought home the troubled, needy kids; the ones from split or abusive homes; the ones whose parents did drugs or drank heavily. She always believed her parents and God could help. Jenny accepted Christ as her Savior at the tender age of four and was steadfast with her faith and trust in Him even through the difficult teen years. It didn't surprise Joshua and Liz that upon her graduation she announced her intention to attend a three year Bible College. Once that was completed, she joined a mission to work with inner city children in Chicago, Illinois. It was hard for them to let her go, but both knew it was her heart's desire. It comforted them to see God's obvious hand on the decision – for her needed monthly support came in rapidly. So, committing their precious only daughter into the Lord's loving care, they prayed with Jenny and sent her off to the Chicago jungle. She'd now been there over two years and was being used mightily to touch hearts and change lives for the Lord Jesus Christ.

After reminiscing about his three children, Joshua changed his mind deciding Jenny would be the first one he'd call. He buzzed the nurse, who arrived shortly to dial the number for him.

Thirty-five minutes later he set the phone down.

Like a typical female, Jenny had wanted to know every detail. Normally, he'd have been a bit put out with her being so detail oriented, but today it helped to speak the words out loud. The two of them had moments of tears together and at one point Jenny had grown very quiet. Thinking the connection had been lost, Joshua said, "Jenny, Jenny, are you there?"

"I'm here dad. I was just thinking." She paused then stated firmly, "Dad, I'm coming."

"Jen, honey . . . your mom just got into the recovery room and could be there for a . . . a while. There might be a more important . . ." Unable to finish, Joshua's voice broke.

"Dad," she said gently yet with growing conviction. "Dad, I need to come for me, and . . . for you." She paused to let that sink in. "Besides, Mom needs to hear our voices. You know that."

Glad she'd insisted, Joshua was relieved to hear she'd be leaving within a couple hours. "I have a couple activities I need to ask other missionaries to take over for me, not to mention packing. I might be there a while, so I want to plan accordingly."

The line grew silent.

Then, Joshua heard Jennifer cautiously ask, "Have you been in contact with Seth?"

Sighing heavily, Joshua replied, "Not yet. You were the first one I called. I plan to call Tony next, and then Seth."

"It'll be all right, Dad. I know it will. Meanwhile, I'm going to call him too. He needs to come! Mom needs to hear all our voices! She needs to know we're all there praying for her." Not hearing a reply from her Dad, Jenny added quietly but with conviction, "That's what we do, Dad. We, Warner's are one unit for the Lord Jesus Christ, even our confused, black sheep, Dad. I have total confidence that someday Seth will get his thinking straight." She paused then said in a half-whisper, "Who knows . . . maybe this is what's needed to show him Christ truly is alive and real."

The two finished their call by having prayer together, and then Joshua tearfully said what he always did at the end of their conversations. "Drive safely, sweetheart. Stay focused on the Lord. I love you, but He loves you even more."

As she rang off, Joshua was surprised at how tired he suddenly felt. It distressed him. He didn't want anything to hinder his calling his sons, nor keep him from seeing his Lizzie.

Asking his nurse to please bring another cup of coffee, Joshua then thought on his second born son once more. It caused his heart to ache. Somewhere along the way he and Elizabeth had made mistakes with Seth. It had to be their fault, right? And yet, they'd raised him the same as the other two.

Joshua's thoughts went on to all the discussions, even arguments he and Liz had gone through over this son. As they had looked back over his high school years, the two of them could now see how Seth had willingly been involved in all the church activities and yet, it never really seemed to touch his heart. It was all head knowledge, and possibly because he knew it was expected of him.

They assumed wrongly that he would straighten out and follow the examples of his siblings. The image of Seth coming to their home and setting them down in the living room was vividly imprinted on Joshua's brain even though it had been over three years earlier. He'd come to announce that he'd quit his job and was going to see and experience the United States. He then shocked them by adding that he was leaving the next morning for California to begin his adventure. Over the past three years, they'd seen him twice; both times ended with harsh words and shortened visits. It was hard to see their son looking grungy and unkempt. He seldom shaved or cut his hair. Joshua knew Seth also tried to cover the fact that he smoked, but couldn't hide the smell on his clothes. In spite of their heartache at Seth openly turning away from what they valued most in life, Joshua and Elizabeth repeatedly let him know that their doors were always open and that they loved him. Joshua believed Seth was uncomfortable around them so his son would pick a fight to have an excuse to leave.

Joshua leaned his head back into the pillow and stared at the ceiling. The last time they'd seen Seth was three months earlier. He'd arrived unannounced and was agitated and argumentative; more so than normal. During supper that night, he was so unlike himself that Liz had asked him if he was doing drugs. Seth never answered; instead he grew angry to the point of raising his voice to Liz. Joshua had never tolerated the kids being disrespectful to their Mother, so had intervened by telling his son to either calm down or leave.

He left.

They didn't hear from him for weeks, until late one night he called. Joshua was surprised to hear a relaxed voice; one they hadn't heard for years. Seth didn't talk long. He mainly wanted to give them his Tracfone number in case they needed to call. Once Joshua heard Seth's voice, he'd pushed the speaker button so Elizabeth could listen in. She'd remained quiet until Seth started saying he had to run; then she quickly asked, "Where are you son?"

Before replying to her question, he'd said, "Hi, Mom. How are you?"

"I'm good, son; but I miss you."

Seth had paused then replied in a lowered, hesitant voice, "I miss you, too; and you . . . Dad."

Joshua had smiled but remained silent so Liz could talk.

Again she'd asked, "Where are you, Seth? What are you doing?"

"I'm in North Dakota. I've gotten a job helping a ranch." He grew silent, then quietly added, "You'd like it here, Mom. This ranch houses a herd of adopted wild mustangs. They are spirited and have lots of space to run."

Joshua remembered how he'd smiled at the way Elizabeth's face had lit up at the mention of the horses. The whole family was very aware of her love for horses and how she'd always wanted one of her own… that thought brought Joshua abruptly back to the present and he made a decision right there and then.

Committing it to the air around him, Joshua vowed, "Lizzie, if you survive this accident, I'm going to buy you a horse!"

His mind being made up, Joshua buzzed for the nurse's help once more. She punched in Seth's number, but all they got was his answering machine. Leaving a note for him to call, Joshua then had her phone Tony, who promptly stated that he'd be there within the hour.

Tired to the bone, Josh weakly smiled at the nurse thanking her for all her help, then snuggled down for another nap. He wanted to be fresh and ready whenever it came time to possibly go see his Lizzie.

The nurse dimmed the lights and softly left the room.

As Joshua's mind tried to settle down for a nap, he felt a strong need to pray for his precious wife and wayward son. *Lord Jesus, please have Seth call. I need to hear his voice. His Momma needs to hear his voice.*

He squeezed his eyes tight as tears began falling once more.

Suddenly, the door popped open and the nurse walked briskly back into the room with her face wreathed in smiles. She promptly turned the lights back on.

As Joshua squinted in the sudden light, he noticed another person entering the room. Once his eyes adjusted, he realized it was a grey haired woman and she was pushing a wheelchair.

"Time to get up, Mr. Warner. You have a date to see a special woman on the third floor!" The elderly aide announced happily. Then with an apology she handed him a sealed plastic bag. "I'm sorry it's taken us so long to get your wife's personal belongings to you. They were misplaced and forgotten for a while. The nurse asked me to explain that your wife's ring and bracelet on her right arm had to be cut off. The parts are in the bag. Also, inside the bag you can see a crumpled photo. Apparently your wife was still clutching it when she arrived in ER. Thinking it might be important, they stuck it in the bag too."

All the time she'd been chattering, the aide was busy helping Joshua up and into the wheelchair.

Satisfied he was secure and his broken arm was snug against him, she noted he was still holding the plastic bag. "Would you like to leave it on the stand while we're gone?"

Holding it tightly with his good hand, Joshua shook his head. He wanted to pull each item out and study it, but not now. He would wait until he could do it alone. Until then, it comforted him to have it in his possession.

CHAPTER EIGHT

As Joshua and the gray-haired escort waited for the hospital elevator, his eldest son Tony walked up to place a hand on his left shoulder.

"Hey, Dad, where you headed?"

"Up to see your mother. It's my first opportunity."

"Mind if I tag along?"

With sad eyes, Joshua readily agreed, but added, "I'm not sure how close they'll let us get, but I'd love your company."

The elevator doors opened just as Joshua was asking the lady of the wheelchair if his son could take over.

"Sure, Mr. Warner. I have another patient needing to be pushed to x-ray. Just take this to the third floor, and then go left. At the end of the hall are the locked doors to the CCU. On the wall is a phone. They're expecting you, so just tell them your name. If your wife is still somewhat stable they'll unlock the doors for you. Stop at the nurses station right inside."

As she spoke, Tony held the elevator doors open and she backed Joshua in. Then patting his shoulder she said, "Good luck Mr. Warner. I hope all goes well with your wife."

"Luck doesn't have anything to do with it," Joshua firmly stated.

To which, Tony quickly added, "My Dad isn't meaning to sound harsh, but we don't believe in luck. We believe in the Lord Jesus Christ. My mom's in His hands; whatever the future holds for her, He will give us the grace and strength to deal with it."

Not saying a word, the woman pasted a weak smile on her face as the doors closed.

Tony sighed heavily, and then said while punching the third floor button, "I guess we could have handled that a little better. By the looks of her face, I think she believes in something other than God."

Having started on the fifth floor, the two men expected the elevator to head down, but instead it continued upward. Resigned to a little delay to their intended destination, Tony stared into the worried eyes of his father. "Dad, have you heard something about Mom since I was here the first time?"

Hours earlier having received the call from the EMT about his parents accident, Tony had gone to the Sr. Pastor to inform him of the situation. The two had prayed and then Tony hurried to the hospital. He arrived there shortly after his parents, but wasn't allowed in to see either of them. Anxious, he'd paced the waiting room area praying fervently until an intern finally came stating his mom was taken to surgery and that his father would soon follow. At that point, Tony insisted on seeing his father a couple minutes first; being reassured that his father's situation wasn't life threatening and that it would be hours before word came of his mother, Tony had left to finish up some errands.

Now, he was back and obviously his mom's surgery was done and she was where they could have some access to her.

It was his father's face that was causing him great concern. Always over the years he had been the strong spiritual leader who had been the glue holding the family together in the midst of difficult times. Now, for the first time Tony saw doubt and fear which was very unsettling. Not getting an immediate response to his question and experiencing a funny feeling in his stomach, Tony grasped at something to temporarily divert his and his dad's thoughts elsewhere.

"So, have you heard from Seth yet?"

Joshua cocked his head slightly Tony's way, bit his lower lip and then said in a tired voice, "No . . . no word, as yet."

A bile of anger rose in Tony's gut toward his wayward younger brother. He started to say something negative, but right then the elevator stopped on the seventh floor and three people came on board. Tony smiled absently as he moved his dad to make more room. As the doors slid shut once more his mind traveled back to a distant memory.

He was six and a new baby had just been brought into the home. Even at that young age, Tony remembered the mixed feelings inside over the fact his beloved mom's time was now taken up with two infants – two year old Jenny and now the newborn, Seth. It hadn't been all that bad when Jenny came along because she was a happy, good baby; but Seth had come in the world colicky and fussy. He demanded lots of his mom's time. Then added to that – one day soon after Seth's entrance to the home, Dad had come in the house, loaded up the television, and carted it away. Tony had liked his morning cartoons and the fun of shooting bad guys with his plastic gun while watching Gunsmoke and Bonanza. His mom had tried explaining the need of money for bills, but the reality couldn't quite seep in to his young brain. Later some friends had given them a used one, but during the interval Tony's mind had coupled the lost television with Seth and that had begun building a seed of resentment in Tony's young heart.

At the ninth floor, two more passengers boarded and then the elevator headed down. Tony heard his father greet the newcomers, but Tony chose to ignore them. Instead, he purposely allowed his already embittered heart to fill with anger toward Seth's once again lack of concern for his precious parents. Setting his feet and standing a little taller, Tony decided then and there it was time little brother realized what his responsibilities were toward his parents. As the past injustices from his brother swirled around and around in Tony, he began feeling more and more that Seth's rebellious attitude deserved any bad thing that came his way.

A short time later the elevator arrived at the third floor. As the doors rolled smoothly open Tony had himself convinced that his brother had better contact his family soon . . . or else!

Having settled that in his mind, Tony suggested the two of them have a time of prayer together before picking up the phone on the wall near the ominously closed CCU doors.

Pamela Bush

CHAPTER NINE

When Elizabeth opened the door, she was surprised to find Joshua standing there. With a dish towel in her hand, she stared at him a second before asking in a slightly confused voice, "Did we make a date for this evening, because if we did I seem to have forgotten about it?"

"No . . . no we didn't. I just heard some disturbing news and I . . . umm . . . well . . . I needed to talk to someone about it. I thought maybe we could sit for a while on your front porch."

Elizabeth frowned at Joshua's tone and the haggard look on his usually calm face. Alarm spread through her as she hollered inside that she'd be on the porch with Joshua. With one ear cocked, she waited for an answering reply before draping the dishtowel over the nearest chair and following him out to the porch. Since there wasn't a porch swing, the two sat side by side on the top front step.

She fully expected him to launch into the reason for his sudden visit, but instead he sat staring at some unseen object not saying a word.

This was a side of Joshua she hadn't seen and Elizabeth wondered what possibly could have disturbed him so much. Angling herself against the front porch support, she asked softly, "What is it, Josh? What has you so bothered?"

Joshua took a deep breath, licked his lips and then turned profoundly sad eyes her way. "I heard some really bad news a short while ago. Last night Eddie and a bunch of his friends were out drinking. I don't know where they were at, but apparently they ran into some older, tough guys who had also been drinking. The whole mess of them ended up at the high school parking lot. One thing lead to another and before most of the group knew what was going on Eddie and one of the older guys drove off to play a game of chicken with their cars. They drove to opposite ends of the parking lot, revved their motors, and then floored it heading straight toward each other."

As Joshua paused to gather his thoughts, Elizabeth's breath caught in her throat as the scene vividly played itself out in her mind. Fear crept through her as the vision of what might have happened forced her eyes to widen. Clasping Joshua's arm, she asked in a choked whisper, "What happened, Josh? Was Eddie really that stupid, or was he that drunk?"

Anger leapt out of Joshua toward the foolishness of Eddie's actions as he grimly stated, "I would say he was both!" Joshua hadn't intended to respond quite that vehemently and when he saw Liz's eyes dilate even wider, he took a deep breath to calm himself and reached for her hand. It was cold, so he began massaging it as he continued with the story.

"According to what was told me, neither one backed off until the last second. When they tried to veer away they'd chosen the same direction. Within seconds both vehicles had flipped and Eddie's did a cartwheel before landing upside down on the tarmac."

"Oh, Joshua! Is Eddie alright?"

Her eyes widened as Joshua sadly shook his head and rubbed his eyes before stating, "Both the guys were killed."

Elizabeth's hand flew to her mouth as she uttered, "No!" Then for the first time a new thought hit her. Turning toward Joshua, she roughly grabbed the front of his t-shirt. "Joshua, did they have passengers with them? Tell me Tilly wasn't with him!!"

"She was there, Liz."

At his words, one of Elizabeth's hands released him to cover her eyes. It was as if she was trying to shut out the horrible scene playing out in her mind. Not looking at him, she whispered,

"Tell me she's okay. Oh, Joshua, Tilly wasn't . . . wasn't..." Unable to finish the horrible thought, Elizabeth slowly lowered her now shaking hand. With tears forming in her eyes, she willed him to continue.

"No, honey. No, she's fine. Well . . . at least she wasn't in the car with Eddie. But as to how fine she is? I imagine right now she's a mess and probably in a boatload of trouble."

He reached again for both of Elizabeth's hands. Holding them firmly in his own, he added, "I was told she'd been drinking and riding around with Eddie all evening. But, surprisingly, when he wanted her to be his passenger for the chicken show down, she'd adamantly refused. Witnesses said Eddie had gotten quite ugly with her over it, but for the first time that I know of . . . she'd stuck with her decision which added fuel to his already drunken state."

"Poor Tilly. She must be overwhelmed with grief and how terrible that it all happened right in front of her."

Suddenly, Elizabeth released Joshua's hands and jumped to her feet. "I must go to her. Do you know where she is?"

Joshua also came to his feet and stopped her pacing with one hand on her shoulder. With the other he gently pulled her chin up so he could look directly into her eyes. "Lizzie, I know where Tilly is, but you won't be able to go see her."

"Why not? She needs her friends right now!" As the urgency of the situation hit her, Elizabeth moved to pull away, but

Joshua's hands held firm.

"Liz . . . you can't go because she's been arrested."

"What?"

"Well, not arrested exactly, but since hanging with Eddie she's been warned several times about being caught drinking. This time the police meant business. Tilly is being detained in a special part of the jail for female minors. She goes before the judge sometime next week."

Joshua paused once more, and then with a voice laced with compassion mixed with anger, he added, "It sounds like she's going to be sent to a juvey center for troubled girls."

At his last pronouncement, all the wind escaped from Elizabeth's body and she sagged back down to the top step once more.

Joshua stared down at her a long moment. He watched Elizabeth shake her head in frustration. When sadness and despair over all he'd just told her filled Liz's face, Joshua sighed heavily and sat down beside her.

Josh's news had been devastating to Elizabeth, but in spite of that, something else he'd let slip was now attempting to capture her attention. He'd called her – honey. Guilt spread through Liz to think that in the midst of such tragedy she was wanting to dwell instead on him saying such an endearing word to her. *But, he called me honey! That must mean he has some affection for me stronger than friend,* she reasoned. Throwing him a happy sideways glance, Liz was promptly brought back to the moment and Josh's news. All thoughts of Joshua fled as Liz's mind filled with pictures of the terrible accident and Tilly sitting in jail.

The silence grew heavy around the two.

They sat there thinking their own thoughts for several minutes until Joshua broke it with, "It seems like such a waste to me."

"Me, too."

Their words were followed by another prolonged period of silence before Joshua broke it once more.

"As I think about the senseless things that happened last night, the thing that has been really bugging me is the thought that there's got to be something more than this."

"I don't understand, Joshua. What do you mean?"

Instead of answering right away, Joshua cocked his head upward to stare into the sky. It being mid-August there weren't any stars in the night sky yet. But, as Liz studied his upturned face, she raised an eyebrow. Josh's stare wasn't looking for stars, it was like he was searching far deeper and further to some object beyond the stars. His steady gaze drew her own eyes skyward. The two of them silently studied the sky as fluffy clouds drifted by; the sun lowered a little more toward the west; and the occasional jet left streaks in the jet stream high above.

Finally deciding there weren't any answers up there for her, Liz brought her disappointed, frustrated eyes downward to find Joshua staring at her. He held her gaze for a long, long moment before taking her hands and saying in a solemn serious voice, "Liz, there has to be more to life than living for the moment and drinking, or drugs, or whatever . . . and I think it somehow has to do with God and knowing Him better."

As he spoke, his voice became stronger with conviction which Liz saw plainly written on his face. It was as if he'd come to some kind of a decision and suddenly a new fear entered her heart as she stared at him.

"In fact Liz, according to most preachers this life is only a small, small portion of eternity."

Still holding her hands, Joshua's eyes traveled back up to the sky above. "Lizzie, do you believe in heaven and hell?"

Elizabeth's heart lurched in her chest at his words and she became increasingly uneasy. With a frown now knitting her brow, she replied, "I don't know. To be honest, I've never really thought about it."

That brought his eyes back to hers. "You've never thought about it? What about God? Surely you've thought about Him?"

"Well . . . yes, sure. I've thought about God, but hasn't everyone?"

"I don't know, Lizzie. I really don't."

Growing more earnest, he gently squeezed her hands and asked, "Liz, will you go to church with me this Sunday?"

That brought Liz's heart all the way up into her throat. It was time to change the subject. Extracting her hands from his, she quickly got to her feet. Walking to the porch railing, she clutched it with her hands as he walked up close beside her.

"What is it, Lizzie? Did I say something wrong? What bothers you about going to church?"

"Well . . . for one thing we're not a church going family. Other than the occasional vacation bible schools I attended as a child, we only go to church for funerals and weddings. The cousins I've been spending this summer with, are the same way."

Once the words were airborne, Liz considered how they sounded and before Joshua could reply she turned her head toward him to say defensively, "Not that we're heathens or anything! Instead, I'd say we're basically good, moral people. My Mom doesn't drink or smoke and my Dad only drinks for special occasions. As for smoking, Dad prefers an evening pipe." She then shrugged to add lamely before looking back over the front yard, "We've never really needed church."

Fully noting her tense posture and nervous attitude, Joshua draped his right arm across Elizabeth's back to snug her close. In her ear he said softly, "Relax, sweetie. I'm the last person to be talking to anyone about heaven and hell, but there's something nagging at me in my insides; something itching to get out. To be honest, I think it's time I investigated God and the Bible to see if they have the answers to my inner questions as to what we're really here for and what else we could be doing that would be more fulfilling."

With his other hand, Joshua slowly brought Liz's face toward his. "Lizzie, I'm sorry to bring you the news about Eddie and Tilly. It's all such a waste!"

Not saying a word, Elizabeth nodded her agreement as she stared into Josh's warm, reassuring hazel eyes which were only inches from her.

"All I'm asking you to do is go with me to church and let's check it out . . . see what it's all about. What do you say?"

Instead of answering, Elizabeth found herself distracted by Joshua's mouth and nearness. He may have been thinking on God and church, but at that moment Liz's body was experiencing strange things. Her heart did a couple flips which caused her pulse to shoot up; as she grew more and more aware of his body so close to hers. A flush of warmth began a slow creep up her arms, crossed her back, and then started up her neck and face. A part of Elizabeth strongly wanted to lean in to feel the warmth of his lips on hers, but another part was trying desperately to not let Joshua see how strongly he was affecting her. Before doing something to embarrass herself, Elizabeth made a move to break the spell and the first thing she could think of was about church. Hurriedly, she stated, "Sure, Josh, I'll go to church with you."

"That's my girl," Joshua said softly in her ear as he peeled one of her clenched hands off the railing. Bringing it to his lips, he added, "Thanks for listening and saying you'll try going to church with me. You're one in a million, Lizzie."

As his warm lips touched her skin, Lizzie closed her eyes to better give herself to the moment, but then she frowned as her hand was suddenly free from any human contact. Instead of Joshua's warm lips on her hand, Elizabeth's hand suddenly felt cold and stiff. Opening her eyes, confusion clouded her mind . . . for Joshua was no longer there.

Frantic, Elizabeth's eyes covered the porch and then swung to the yard and street beyond.

He was nowhere in sight!

With heart racing out of control and a cloud of confusion filling her mind, Elizabeth ran through her cousin's house, but he wasn't there either!

Joshua had disappeared into thin air and no matter how hard she tried, Elizabeth couldn't find him anywhere!

CHAPTER TEN

When the nurse told Joshua there wasn't room in the cubicle for his wheelchair and that he'd have to be content stationed at the end of Liz's bed, Joshua's commanding presence showed itself. Insisting there wasn't anything wrong with his legs, he proved the point by coming to a stand.

At first the nurse grew indignant, but then conceded the point. Having only one free hand, Joshua laid the still unopened bag of Lizzie's things in the wheelchair seat and then walked up to lay eyes for the first time on his Lizzie. His breath caught in his throat at sight of her. The tubes and machines all around didn't register as his focus zeroed in on his beloved Lizzie's face. None of her wonderful features were recognizable . . . for her face was severely swollen and bruised; especially the right side. Oxygen was being piped into her nostrils, her mouth was slightly open and her lips were dry and already cracking. Searching the nearby stand, Joshua found moist "lollipop" sticks used for that very purpose. Picking one up, he carefully rubbed it over her pale, swollen lips; all the while his heart was aching at sight of her.

A lump choked his throat as silent tears made their way down his cheeks. Blinking them away, Joshua gently lifted her lifeless left hand into his. It being the one housing the IV, he wasn't able to stroke it as he wanted, but he could lay it flat on his own warm one. As he did, Joshua studied the pale, unresponsive fingers and his heart broke all over again.

"Oh, Lizzie, my dear, dear Lizzie," he groaned over and over again as he felt his son's strong hand grip his shoulder.

Without taking his eyes from Liz's face, Joshua said with a catch, "Son . . . I've stood where you are countless times trying to strengthen, pray, and support others in this same situation; but until this very moment I didn't really . . . didn't truly understand what was going on inside of them."

He took a quick breath and then finished with a cracked voice laced with tears, "This is so hard to see. I feel so helpless!"

For a moment, Tony feared his Dad would break down. As unreasonable as it seemed . . . he needed his Dad to be strong right now. He needed his Dad to show him how to cope with the horrible sight of his Mom lying there battered, swollen, and broken with casts on her right leg from thigh to toe and another on her right arm and wrist. The sight was overpowering Tony's senses. If his Dad fell apart; so would he.

But then Tony felt his Dad straighten under the grip on his shoulder and he heard him say with a determined voice, "This isn't the time or place to feel sorry for ourselves. Lizzie needs us to be confident and encouraging. She needs us to talk positively whenever we're within her hearing. But, most of all son, she needs to hear our love and prayers for her."

Joshua then turned his head to stare directly into his son's eyes. "And . . . under no circumstances are we to talk about her condition or how she looks while standing near her!"

Before Tony could respond, a doctor walked up to check Elizabeth's vitals and study the nearby computer information. He then turned to Joshua. "The nurse said you're the patient's husband and son. I'm one of her physician's. May I have words with you?"

"Sure, doctor. Where would you like to do that?"

"There's a private conference room off the waiting room. If you don't mind, I'd like to talk there."

When Tony helped his Dad back into the wheelchair he noted the bag his father picked up and held close to his chest. He started to ask about it, but decided it wasn't the time. A few moments later, the three men were stationed in the small, impersonal conference room. Fleetingly, Tony wondered how many people had heard bad news in that same room, but brought his mind back to attention when the doctor began speaking.

"Gentlemen, Ms. Warner's condition is very grave. I know you may have been told some of her problems, but so I know you're up to speed, I'm going to go over them again."

"That's okay, doctor. My son, Tony, wasn't there for the first briefing and I haven't had a chance to fill him in. Go ahead."

Tony nodded in agreement.

"Well, as you already noted she has casts on. Her leg was fractured in two places, but they were clean breaks and she has good bones. They look to have set well. The same goes for her arm and wrist. She also has a hairline fracture in her collarbone, but that's not a priority so nothing was done. The seatbelt bruised her chest and broke a couple ribs, but again the ribs aren't causing her undue lung stress so they aren't a priority either.

"She does have a bruised spleen which has caused some abdominal edema. At this moment the swelling hasn't increased, so isn't a great concern. It is being monitored, though." He paused a moment to make sure the men were paying close attention and then went on. "Our main concern is the head injury. The extensive swelling has made it difficult for us to ascertain the extent of the damage. The good news is that she's breathing on her own, which is a very good sign. Because of the head injury, in a few hours we plan to do a scan to check for any possible brain bleeds."

To which Joshua urgently asked, "Why not do it now? Wouldn't it be better to know in case something could be done?"

"We've tried . . . but the swelling is throwing the image off. We think the trauma of the accident is still playing a major role in hindering us. She's heavily sedated and we want to give her body a few hours to calm down. Hopefully then we'll be able to get a better read. If not, we'll keep trying every couple hours or so until we can get an accurate picture of what's going on."

The doctor stared at the two men again. Then said, "I know this is a lot to take in . . . but I do have some good news for you. Mr. Warner, your wife appears to have been a fairly healthy woman. Her bone density is strong for her age which will promote good healing; also her vitals are stable. As long as they remain so, she has a very good chance of pulling through this."

When he saw the men getting hopeful, the doctor quickly cautioned, "But men, you must understand . . . the next 24 to 36 hours are crucial. If she survives those, she has a fighting chance; but will still be facing months of recovery and therapy."

While the doctor had been talking, Joshua's mind often pictured Elizabeth's battered state and he had some questions. When it appeared the doctor was done with his briefing, Joshua asked, "My wife is so still. Is she in a coma?"

"No, she's not. We've heavily sedated her. That's to help

her cope with the intense pain she'd be feeling with less medication."

"Why the oxygen? You said she's breathing on her own."

"With the amount of medication she's being given intravenously, it has slowed her heart rate and breathing. The oxygen is to make sure she gets the necessary oxygen she needs and to make it easier for her to rest."

At that point, the doctor checked his watch and then came to a stand; he extended his hand. "Gentlemen, she needs you to talk positive when you're around her and starting now . . . for the next day or so, visitors will be limited to one per hour for only five minutes. Any further questions for me?"

Joshua thought for a moment and then said, "Just one more question, doctor. I noticed that even though Lizzie's non-responsive, her eyes seemed to be moving a lot. It was noticeable even through the swelling."

For the first time the doctor smiled. "They are, huh? I hadn't noticed, but that's actually good news. If that's true . . . it means your wife has good, functioning brain activity."

Tony piped up with, "Is Mom distressed? Is she fretting or feeling pain? Is that why her eyes are moving?"

"No. If I were to make an educated guess . . . I'd say your mother is dreaming."

He turned to leave when Joshua extended his left hand.

"Thank you, doctor. Thank you for all you're doing for my wife."

The doctor gave him a firm shake, and then did the same for Tony. "You're welcome." He opened the door, but before walking out he paused to say, "Your wife, and mother is in the Lord's hands. Trust Him."

He then exited and closed the door behind him.

Startled at his last words, Joshua and Tony stared at the door and then turned toward each other. In spite of all they'd just heard about Elizabeth's condition and how crucial the next two days were . . . the doctor's parting words were a welcome comfort.

Not being able to visit Elizabeth again for almost an hour, the two men solemnly made their way to Joshua's room.

Once there, Tony helped his Dad stand beside the hospital bed and then pulled the wheelchair away so he could get back into the bed. Joshua set the bag on the nearby stand and then beckoned his son closer in order to put his good arm around his shoulder. As best he could, Joshua hugged him close. Knowing they were both experiencing the same doubts and fears, Joshua said while climbing back into the bed, "Son, the doctor's words are true and right. She is in the Lord's hands and we need to trust that whatever He has planned for her and us . . . is the best."

A few moments later, a nurse showed up to check Joshua's vitals.

Confident his father was settled and in need of a nap, Tony

said he'd be back later that evening and left.

When Joshua woke up a couple hours later, he was happy to see Jenny seated nearby reading a book; but was chagrined to find he'd slept two and a half hours.

Seeing her father finally awake, Jenny walked close to plant a kiss on his cheek. "Hey, Dad, how are you feeling?"

"Emotionally drained and a little sore, but I'm not complaining." He pushed the bed button to raise himself into a sitting position. "How long have you been here?"

Jenny glanced at the wall clock. "Oh, about forty-five minutes. You were sleeping so soundly, I let you be." Then pointing with her finger, she stated, "I brought you something."

Joshua swiveled his head, stared at the bedside stand, and then chuckled. "Leave it to my daughter!"

What he saw was a colorful weighted ball sporting a three foot fishing pole sticking out of the top of it. Suspended on a string from the pole was a plastic old-fashioned biplane. Dangling from the bottom wing was a man holding on for dear life with his hands. Tied to his foot was a small banner reading, "Hang in there. Get well soon!"

Still smiling, Joshua brought his eyes back to his one and only daughter, his middle child . . . Jennifer. He stared lovingly at her a moment before saying, "Thanks, kiddo."

Jennifer jumped to help him straighten his pillow and then

offered his water for a couple sips. Once settled back, he asked, "Have you been to see your mother?"

She glanced again at the clock before responding. "They said I could in about ten minutes; but now that you're awake, maybe you should go instead."

To which Joshua promptly shook his head. "Thanks, but I think you need to see her. So you should go this time."

She started to protest, but then relented to ask, "Dad, will you go with me?"

"I can't go in, but sure . . . I'll go. I can wait for you up there just as well as here." So saying, he buzzed the nurse, but as he did one walked in to say, "Mr. Warner, I have good news! You're doing so well, the doctor said you can be released from the hospital later this evening."

For a moment, the two already in the room froze; unsure of how to respond. Joshua's only thought was that he wouldn't be near his Lizzie now.

Apparently thinking the same, Jenny asked the nurse, "Don't you have a hospitality house or some place Dad can stay to be close to Mom?"

"Sure, we do! In fact let me call them right now." The nurse picked up the phone and continued with, "These rooms fill up quickly, so let's make sure one is available."

Within a couple minutes the room was reserved.

Thankful, Joshua asked the nurse about letting him go with Jenny to the third floor to see his Lizzie again. The nurse took time to check his vitals once more and then left to find a wheelchair.

A short time later, he was back out of the wheelchair stationed on a couch in the waiting room holding a steaming cup of hot coffee; while Jenny was ushered into the CCU to see her mother for the first time.

Five minutes later, Jenny walked back into the waiting room.

Noting the look on her face, Joshua sat his coffee down and came to his feet. Within seconds, Jenny was held close by his good arm as she cried against his shoulder. Before going in, he had tried warning Jenny as to her mother's condition, but no words could truly prepare anyone for the busted up condition of a loved one.

Since other people were in the room with them, Joshua considered stepping out into the hall with her; but then reasoned that everyone was probably experiencing the same kind of feelings. So . . . he slowly lowered both their bodies back on to the couch and continued holding Jenny until the storm had stopped.

When she finally lifted her head, a kind woman handed them a box of tissue.

Joshua noticed the woman's eyes were suspiciously wet and mouthed a thank you as he pulled a couple from the box.

"Dad, she looks terrible! I couldn't even recognize her!" Jenny blew her nose and hiccupped a couple times between the sentences.

"I know, sweetheart. I'm sorry."

He waited for her to take a couple deep breaths and blow her reddening nose again, before asking, "How is she? Did the nurse by chance talk to you?"

"I don't know how she is. No one talked to me, but just as I bent to kiss her hand a technician walked up with some kind of portable machine." Jenny paused, gave a heavy sigh and then added, "As I turned to leave, he told me they were doing a brain scan on Mom."

Joshua nodded his head at her words. "The doctor said they'd be doing those regularly; at least until they can get a clear picture of her brain. They want to see if your Mom has any brain bleeds going on."

"Brain bleeds? That doesn't sound good. What happens if they do?"

"I honestly don't know, Jenny." At that, Joshua got to his feet and pulled her up with him. "What I do know is . . . I want to get changed and situated in the hospitality house before our next visiting time. Come on, sweetheart. There's nothing more we can do here for now. We're both mentally and emotionally tired. Let's go back to my room. I'm not sure when the doctor will let me go, but I want to be there when he comes in."

CHAPTER ELEVEN

"So, what did you think?"

Joshua Warner and Elizabeth English were walking hand in hand through the park. It was a beautiful, sunshiny Sunday and they'd just attended their first church service together. Elizabeth had been hesitant about going for she saw herself as a good girl not in need of formalized religion, but Joshua had been persuasive about his need to attend and wanting her with him.

So, she'd agreed.

Now, he was wondering what she thought and Elizabeth was having a hard time formulating the words.

"Well, Lizzie, what did you think?" He asked again. "Did you like it? What did you think about his talk on heaven and hell?"

While talking, Joshua had spied a nearby bench and had angled her toward it while enthusiastically bombarding her with more questions.

Taking a seat beside him, Elizabeth felt her defenses rise up as he turned sideways to take both her hands in his. "Didn't his words make your heart and mind leap at times?"

When Elizabeth was young, she developed a fear of spiritual things that wasn't just limited to God . . . it also included the world of evil. Somewhere along the line, she'd come to believe that evil spirits really existed and they scared her. When High School came along that fear became amplified through the means of slumber parties.

Now as Elizabeth tried gathering her thoughts to answer Joshua, her mind traveled to slumber parties with youthful attempts at levitation and Ouija boards. Her friends always wanted Liz to be involved because somehow the things seemed to work when she was.

The truth was that Elizabeth was scared half out of her mind to the point whenever those kinds of activities started, she'd hurry from the room. Her friends would find her talking with the parents or watching television. Strangely, as Elizabeth thought on it, her friends had never condemned her or made fun because she'd left the room. Instead, her popularity seemed to grow and she was invited to most everyone's home for parties.

From these scary experiences, Elizabeth's mind had joined the evil with the good and all of it was fearful to her. She wanted to leave all of it alone, including things pertaining to God.

"Elizabeth, are you alright? You look scared. What's going on?"

She raised eyes to Joshua's warm hazel ones and a feeling of safety flowed through her at the concern and strength she saw reflected in them. Finally finding her voice, she said, "I didn't like the preacher's looks. He greases his hair, of all things! Should a preacher do that?"

At her words, Joshua's eyebrows arched in surprise and then he broke into laughter.

Not sure what was so funny, Elizabeth stiffened and tried pulling her hands away from his warm ones, but was held fast.

"Oh, Lizzie, you are definitely one in a million! Of all the things to walk out of church thinking about, you are unhappy with the preacher's hairstyle." He chuckled again.

Once he'd put it that way, Elizabeth couldn't help but bring a quirky smile to her own lips. "I guess it does sound a little silly, huh?"

"Yes, yes it does." Releasing one hand, Joshua gently stroked one of her cheeks while adding, "But, Lizzie, it's that part of you that makes you so cute and lovable."

Catching her breath, she whispered, "Am I lovable?"

Joshua stared deeply into her large blue eyes. "You're absolutely adorable!"

His hand moved to Liz's long hair and he fingered some strands. "I've always been a sucker for blue eyes, freckles, and auburn hair that glistens like it's highlighted with gold."

Drawing his eyes back to her reddening face, he said in a deeper voice, "You couple all that with a wonderful personality and you get quite a powerful package . . . Lizzie."

For an instant Liz thought he meant to kiss her right there in the public park, which prompted her to lick dry lips; but instead he broke the spell by cocking his head slightly and lifting his eyes toward the sky.

He didn't say a word, but Elizabeth's senses were heightened as he caressed the top of her still-held hand with his thumb and continued touching her hair with the other. The strange thing was . . . she wasn't being moved in a sensual way. Instead, it was like . . . it was like his touch was conveying feelings of concern, and even a touch of love all mingled in a respectful spiritual way.

Elizabeth stared at his upturned face. For the first time she openly entertained the thought that she was developing special feelings for this young man beside her. Up until the last few minutes, Elizabeth knew she enjoyed his company; but in the back of her mind it was always understood that she was in Louisiana for the summer and then heading back to Michigan. Thoughts of a long term relationship hadn't factored in . . . until now. As his last few words played themselves out in her mind, Elizabeth's insides tingled at the thought that maybe, just maybe he was feeling the same for her. These thoughts so engulfed her thinking, that Joshua's next words took a moment to penetrate that fog of wonder.

"Elizabeth, if you can get your thoughts beyond the preacher's looks, what did you think when he said that everyone of us are lost and separated from God; and that the only way to bridge that separation is by believing in the Lord Jesus Christ – God's only Son?"

On the last sentence, Joshua brought his eyes back to Elizabeth's. He went on to say, "You know I've always believed in God." He released her hair to spread his arm out before them. "I mean, honestly, who can look at all this creation and not think there's a Divine Creator somewhere?"

Elizabeth's eyes studied the world around them. The park wasn't all that big but it was beautifully landscaped. A kaleidoscope of colorful flowers bloomed along the walking path; mingled with a variety of shrubs and ferns. As she gazed around her, it became apparent that the focal point of the park was a large, very old looking oak tree situated in the center. It had moss dangling from its massive branches and Elizabeth wondered how old it was.

While she'd been observing her surroundings, Joshua had been studying her expressive face and now said, "See what I mean?

The evidence is everywhere you look!"

Elizabeth brought her eyes back to his. "You're right. All this can't be just an accident; but . . . to say that the only way to God is through belief in Jesus seems very narrow minded to me."

"It might seem that way, but what if he's right? I mean, what if Jesus Christ really is the only true way just like the preacher said? If that could be true, shouldn't we at least check it out for ourselves and find out for sure?"

Joshua grew thoughtful again as he stared at an ant working diligently at the edge of the path. "You know . . . sometimes I feel as insignificant as that ant."

"What do you mean by insignificant?"

"Think about it. Just walking to this bench, I bet we stepped on several if not lots of ants; snuffed out their lives, and didn't even notice."

He studied the ant going in and out of a little hole and then swung his eyes skyward once more. "Everything about our planet and solar system is precise and organized. I once heard a man say that we are exactly the distance from the sun that we need to be to survive on earth. Closer . . . we would burn up; further away . . . we'd freeze!"

Joshua swung his earnest, almost pleading eyes her way. "Lizzie, I for one want to know God in a more personal way. I want to see and experience that 'peace that surpasses all understanding' the preacher talked about today. And . . ." He stopped to fervently take her hands in his warm ones once more, before finishing with, "And . . . I'm hoping you do, too."

CHAPTER TWELVE

After Jenny was sure her Dad was settled once again in his bed, she left him with a long hug and kiss on his cheek. It bothered Jenny the lost puppy look her father had as she turned back at the door to wave good-bye. She'd never seen her father so discouraged and well . . . overwhelmed and Jenny wasn't sure how to deal with it. Besides the strength she daily received from her trust in Jesus Christ and reading his word, her father was her rock. Jenny always knew he had words to guide and encourage her, but now?

Now, he needed someone to do the same for him and Jenny was coming up empty.

As she slowly drove toward her parent's home, Jenny felt a strong desire not to be alone in the house. Various friends to visit flashed across her mind, but at the same time each was checked off . . . too talkative . . . too quiet . . . probably out on a date.

She didn't need a diversion, what Jenny needed was to be with family. After a heavy sigh and a slowing vehicle, Jenny was jolted to a decision when a car horn blew behind her to speed up. She pulled over letting the person-in-a-hurry by, Jenny then turned at the next road to head to her brother Tony's.

Tony wasn't her first choice; that would have been her younger brother, Seth. Even though Seth was the one always getting into trouble while growing up and usually somehow involving her too, he was the one she'd always been closer to. But since she didn't know where he was . . . Tony would have to do.

A couple minutes later she pulled up to his apartment.

~ ~ ~ ~ ~ ~ ~ ~ ~ ~

Joshua watched Jenny leave then stared at the wall for a long time. He was glad the nurse was able to get a room reserved for him at the hospitality house. It would make for fairly easy access to Lizzie . . . if . . . God forbid . . . there should be a need for him to get there quickly.

Frustrated that the doctor had decided to delay his release until the following morning and not liking where his thoughts were headed, Joshua reached for the controls and turned on the television. He randomly clicked through the channels. Nothing caught his attention, so he shut it back off.

Joshua then spied his Bible on the nearby night stand, which Tony had thoughtfully swung to the house to get before coming for his visit that evening. He picked it up to fan the pages; hoping a passage of encouragement would present itself.

None did.

All Joshua could see in his mind was his broken and quiet Lizzie lying so still and alone in the sterile hospital cubicle. From there his thoughts wandered to the still unopened bag of Liz's belongings. Not wanting to attempt getting back out of bed, Joshua buzzed the nurse, who gladly got it out from the cupboard and handed it to him. Thanking her profusely and firmly stating there wasn't anything more he needed, Joshua sighed when the nurse finally left and he could focus on the bag's contents.

Unfortunately, he struggled getting the zip lock bag open, but finally figured out he could tuck it between the cast of his broken arm and his body while doing the zipper with his good left hand. One by one he pulled the items out to take stock of the inventory – the first item pulled out was her wedding ring which he was relieved to see was still intact; then came her watch which was still ticking; a pair of earrings; the necklace he'd bought her for an anniversary; two halves of a ring she often wore on her right hand, and the pieces of a gold bracelet she'd gotten from Jenny one year for Christmas. The only other thing left in the bag was the crumpled picture.

Pulling it out, Joshua carefully tried to smooth it out. He was curious what the photo was about. Once fairly flattened out, Joshua stared at a photo of himself taken in the French Quarters of New Orleans, Louisiana. He looked to be in his late teens, which put the date of the photo in the mid-sixties. As he studied the wrinkled picture, Joshua's own brows furrowed into a frown. Glimpses of Liz holding the photo and them talking about it, surfaced in his brain. Then, little by little the scene played itself fully in Joshua's mind. Up until that moment, he'd been unable to recall exactly what had happened at the time of the accident. But now, the photo brought everything back . . . Liz flipping through the photos his Mom had just given them to take home and scan into their computer . . . Liz wishing she'd known him back then . . . his turning to smile at her words of how handsome he was.

Joshua's thoughts then jumped to the vehicle careening toward them and his body shuddered at the remembrance of seeing the truck ready to hit them and his instinctive move to protect his loved one.

Groaning heavily, Joshua's eyes moistened with tears as he felt a strong need to be by her side. Picking up his buzzer, Joshua called the night nurse. After convincing her of his need to be near Lizzie, Joshua was shortly on his way back to the CCU . . . this time without a wheelchair but with a nurse walking close beside him. Upon their arrival, the nurse left him alone with his beloved for a few precious moments. He stood looking down at his Lizzie; once again gently massaging her good hand with his thumb.

"Hey, sweetheart . . . . I couldn't sleep so thought I'd come by. The nurse was nice and said I could stay a couple minutes, even though it's after visiting hours."

Joshua's voice trailed off as he stared at Lizzie's swollen, misshapen face. Tears threatened, but he held them at bay as he leaned close to plant a kiss on the tip of her nose. He hovered near Liz's ear to whisper, "You're my heart and soul, sweetie. I need you back here with me . . . so fight . . . don't give up . . . okay?"

As Joshua slowly raised his head away, one of his tears escaped and dropped onto her cheek. With infinite love and care, he wiped it off as the nurse's footsteps drew near.

"Mr. Warner, I'm going to have to take you back to your room now."

Joshua straightened, staring at Lizzie; his hand still cradling hers. The feel of her hand reminded him of their little love signal. Suddenly positive he'd get a much needed response from her; Joshua tickled the palm of her hand with one finger . . . then expectantly waited.

Nothing. Lizzie's hand didn't flinch or twitch. It stayed still and motionless.

Saddened, Josh turned to face the nurse. "Thanks for letting me come back. I really . . . really appreciate it."

He slowly laid her hand on the bed then backed away. With

a break in his voice Joshua said to the CCU nurse, "Take good care of her, okay?"

With that he and his nurse companion walked back to his room.

CHAPTER THIRTEEN

(Later that Night)

Seth Warner glanced at his watch. It was almost 1 a.m. and he'd just arrived at the hospital. He still hadn't contacted his family even though he'd received multiple calls on his cell phone.

His intention was to slip in, see his Mom, and then drive away again without anyone of the family knowing of his presence. But now that he was in the hospital parking lot, Seth wasn't sure he was strong enough to see his mother alone.

With everything he'd put his parents through over the last few years, Seth wasn't even sure he had the right to be near her . . . let alone walk in unannounced.

"You probably won't get to see her anyway at this time of night, so turn around and leave," Seth told himself.

But then, something stronger urged him on . . . the need to see for himself just how bad his mother was.

His mother . . . Seth's mind filled with growing up memories and how his Mom factored in. She'd grown up a tomboy, the youngest of six kids. That made her tough and yet . . . fun. She liked making everything an adventure and welcomed their friends whenever they wanted to come around. She even kept extra snacks and drinks in the house just for that purpose. She also loved to laugh; loved music . . . especially the Oldies which often bothered Dad so Mom would crank up the oldies when Dad wasn't home just so they could sing and dance around the house. She liked outdoorsy things like camping and she even used to hunt with Dad during small game and deer season.

Another great thing about his Mom was her availability. She loved talking to Seth and his siblings about their school day.

"We always knew we could come to her about anything. She'd listen, give advice or scripture where needed, or kneel with us and pray for a friend in trouble," Seth voiced to the night air.

His mind moved on to high school and how the once comforting scripture and prayers began bothering Seth. He began questioning the relevance of God and the Bible for today's world. Seth now recalled the pained look on his Mom's face the first time he'd questioned the existence of God. For a moment she'd been speechless and then she'd started to give him proof from the Bible.

Seth hadn't been interested, so tuned her out and shortly found an excuse to go somewhere.

That's when discord in the home really began to surface. Jenny had maintained her relationship with Seth, but Tony had become condemning and critical. So much turmoil built up that the morning after his graduation from high school, Seth packed a bag and left home.

At first, life was a huge adventure and he was free; free to go and do whatever he wanted. Here was Seth's opportunity to see and experience the world.

"I did that all right," Seth stated bitterly to the night. "What a fool I've been!"

Now, sitting in his car in the hospital parking lot, Seth wished he could take back or change so much of the past few years, but knew that was impossible. In spite of his wild ways and the hurts he'd caused his parents, the one thing that had remained constant in the back of Seth's mind was the fact his parents loved him. He replayed his last visit and how his Dad had pretty much kicked him out. Even then, Seth knew his parents did it out of love for him and his lack of respect for them.

Seth sighed heavily and rubbed the memory of that last argument and his Mom's hurting facial expression from his mind.

He took solace in the thought that things were different now. He was different.

The true God of the universe; his parent's first love . . . had gotten a hold of Seth's life once more and that fact is what had driven him hundreds of miles back to Michigan.

Seth needed to let his Mom know.

He sighed again. *I hope it's not too late. I hope she's not in a coma or something and not able to hear my words.*

Suddenly, a long ago conversation with his Dad came to mind. His father had returned from a hospital visit with someone in a coma. When he shared the event with the family, Dad had mentioned taking the man's hand and praying out loud for him.

Young Seth had asked, "Could that man hear you? I thought you said he was in a coma?"

"I believe so, son. The doctors say the hearing is the last sense to go. That's why we need to take care what we say around unconscious or comatose people."

Seth didn't know if his mother was in a coma or not, but the distant memory of that conversation prompted him to open his door and walk toward the security office situated at the hospital Emergency entrance.

He needed access to his Mom's room.

~ ~ ~ ~ ~ ~ ~ ~ ~ ~

Seth tried not to fidget when the guard examined his driver's license then gave him the once over. The man stared hard into Seth's eyes before picking up the phone to punch in some numbers.

When someone at the other end answered, he said, "I have a . . ." he glanced at the license to read, "Seth Alan Warner here. Says he drove in from another state to see his mother who is in CCU."

The officer listened a moment; muttered, "Okay" and hung up.

Still holding the license, he pointed to a nearby chair. "Take a seat. A nurse is on her way down."

About ten minutes later a glass door to Seth's right slid open and a middle aged woman walked through. She paused to scan the scattered other people sitting in the ER waiting room, and then spied Seth by the front entrance.

Walking up to him she asked, "Mr. Warner?"

Seth came to his feet. "Yes, ma'am."

Like the guard, she too took great care studying his appearance and face before asking, "Do you have some form of identification?"

By that time the guard had walked from behind his safety cubicle and was standing nearby. He extended the hand holding Seth's license; which the woman took.

She read the information, and then looked at Seth again. "I understand you drove a long distance to get here."

"Yes, Ma'am, I did and I came directly here upon arrival. I know it's almost 1:30 a.m., but I was hoping you'd let me see my Mom . . . even if it's only a couple minutes."

Seth noted the nurse's eyebrows lift slightly at his involuntary pause after uttering the endearing name, but he didn't press it. Instead, he fell silent . . . waiting.

The woman sighed, looked at the ceiling, then at the security guard.

Seth saw the man give a slight affirmative nod with his head.

The woman directed her eyes back to his. "Young man, this is highly unusual. Normally we don't allow family in during these early hours unless there's a change in the patient . . . which isn't the case here. Your mother is somewhat stable and has been for hours."

That was good news to Seth's ears. Not hearing anything he could really respond to, Seth remained silent; his eyes glued to the pondering woman's face.

He noticed a softening to her stern features when the woman said in a gentler voice, "You do realize that your mother has received substantial damage? Her face is severely swollen and most of her right side is in casts."

Seth briefly closed his eyes trying to shut out the sudden vision assailing his senses. Opening them once more he stated, "That's what my family said. Nurse, umm, what's your name?"

"Nurse Stilson."

"Ms. Stilson, I've driven a lot of miles today. I'm really tired and need to get some sleep. I'm only asking for a couple minutes . . . five at the most."

Then without planning to, Seth did what he hadn't intended… he pleaded, as tears fought to surface. "Please, please. I need to see my Mom. The last time I saw my parents there were . . . words. Words, I greatly regret! Please let me see her."

"Okay, young man," she replied while laying a hand on his shoulder.

She handed him back the driver's license then turned back toward the glass doors.

"Follow me," she commanded.

Twenty-two minutes later a shaken Seth was back in the car.

In spite of the family's and nurse's warnings, the sight of his precious mother was a shock.

Now safely in the privacy of his car, Seth let the tears flow freely while moaning over and over, "Oh, Mom. Why you? That should have been me!"

He pounded the steering wheel for good measure, hoping it would ease the ache surging in his heart.

It didn't help.

Once the tears were spent, Seth wiped his face on his sleeve. He calmed down enough to go over what had transpired while in with his Mom.

After the initial shock, with determination Seth moved closer to her ear. He only had a few minutes and there was much to say.

He told his Mom what a wonderful mother she'd been and

that his wandering away from the beliefs and teachings of the home weren't her or his father's fault.

"Everything was my fault, Mom. It was all me!"

Unaware that he'd spoken the words loud enough for the nurses to hear, Seth went on to tell Elizabeth how sorry he was for all he'd put her through and the heart pain he'd caused. He then told her how the Lord Jesus Christ had lovingly and patiently wooed him back into the Shepherd's fold.

"Mom, I was that one lost sheep, but neither Jesus nor you and Dad gave up on me. Jesus sought me and found me and lovingly forgave me when I finally realized what an absolute fool I've been! What time I've wasted!"

Realizing his time was probably growing short; Seth dashed away his falling tears, took a deep breath and leaned very close to his mother's ear.

"Mom, if you can hear me, please forgive me. And, Mom . . . I need you now more than ever! You need to fight to get back to us! Do you hear me, Mom? Fight! And, please forgive me."

He'd then done something bizarre. Seth asked her to move a finger so he could know she'd heard and forgiven him.

As the nurse walked up to usher him out, Seth fully expected the Lord to allow his Mom's finger to move, but . . . nothing happened.

CHAPTER FOURTEEN

"I can't believe how fast the summer went," Liz moaned while running a hand through her bangs. "It feels like I just got here and now it's time to head back to Michigan!"

While talking she'd been pacing the length of her cousin's front porch, while Joshua half sat on the railing with his back against the corner post.

She came to a stop in front of him and sighed heavily. Fearing tears might pour out if she looked into his wonderful, hazel eyes, Liz stared instead at the neighbor's house across the street. She heard Joshua come to a stand and then felt him at her side, but as much as she longed for him to wrap his arms around her . . . he didn't.

Instead, he softly said, "I know you probably think this isn't going to be hard for me . . . but you'd be wrong. It bothers me a great deal that you're going to be a thousand miles from me and that I won't be able to see you whenever I want."

As he spoke, Liz turned her body toward him. She couldn't help but notice how good he looked in his dark t-shirt and blue jeans, not to mention his lean, healthy body; but what mainly caught her attention was the serious look on his handsome face. It was the most serious she'd seen him. He stood with hands tucked in his front pockets.

Liz openly stared into his eyes, feeling herself falling more and more in love, which made her heart ache even more over the upcoming separation.

Tears threatened once again as he added, "Elizabeth, you've come to mean a lot to me."

Joshua pulled a hand free to begin caressing Liz's cheek with one finger. "Today has been a really great, fun day; one that I will carry with me for a long time."

His finger moved toward her lips. Once there, he lightly tapped them while saying, "Although, I really think you should have told me what an accomplished rider you are before we headed out on our horseback ride this afternoon."

Liz chuckled. All her life she'd wanted to have her own horse, but her family could never afford one. Even so, she'd learned what she could about horses and always jumped at the chance to ride when friends with horses offered.

She'd done the same thing with Joshua when he mentioned his uncle had horses and off they went. Upon their arrival, he'd asked her if she had much experience to which Liz had honestly replied, "Not really." What she failed to mention was that she was a natural and was often told so.

Joshua assumed she was a novice and was concerned about her safety, so he began to explain the basics.

Elizabeth had tried to explain it really wasn't necessary, but Joshua insisted on going over it thoroughly in spite of her protests. And, because she was partial to Appaloosas, he purposely chose one he knew to be gentle and mild. Josh's uncle had greeted them upon their arrival, then had left for an appointment. Unfortunately though, Josh wasn't warned that the black appaloosa had recently developed the bad habit of trying to unseat his riders by going down and attempting to roll them off his back.

They'd started down the field with Elizabeth in the lead on the big Appie, when to Josh's horror, the horse suddenly started to go down. Visions of the large horse rolling over Elizabeth prompted him to dig in his heels on the bay he was riding. The horse responded instantly and charged forward. Joshua's heart raced as he drew close, but then to his amazement, when the appaloosa's knees started buckling Liz smoothly pulled her feet from the stirrups and easily jumped clear of the horse.

Joshua's fear had turned to anger as he sharply reined in next to the now standing Liz and he jumped off his own horse. First he made sure she was fine, then grabbed the Appie's reins and jerked him to a stand. At first the horse wouldn't budge, but when Liz joined in by slapping him on the rump he came to his feet. Soon after he was tied to a nearby sapling, Josh checked the saddle and then tightened the cinch in case anything had broken or loosened. Satisfied all was okay, he then informed Liz they were switching mounts which caused one of their first arguments.

Liz felt capable of handling the horse, but Josh wouldn't hear of it. Finally in exasperation Elizabeth suggested, "Since we're not that far from the barn, let's ride double and lead my horse back to the barn. Then we can get a different one for me."

Agreeing, Joshua untied the horse, looped the Appaloosa's reins over his saddle horn, and then helped Liz up on the bay's rump. Once she was situated close behind him with her arms around his waist, Joshua's serious mood evaporated and he was tempted to do their whole ride that way. But once they started moving and he felt how much Liz was being bounced around he decided that wasn't the best idea; so made his way back to the barn with the troublesome horse in tow.

A short while later they headed out again; this time Liz was on a beautiful buckskin.

That ride had happened hours earlier. After that, they had gone antiquing; where Joshua insisted on buying Elizabeth a beautiful piece of McCoy pottery. Then they had enjoyed supper and a drive-in movie.

Now, they were back at her cousins preparing to say their good-byes; and prolonging it as long as they could.

As the two relived the moment, they both laughed but then Joshua grew serious once more. Placing both hands on her cheeks, he said earnestly, "I'm so glad you came down to Louisiana to spend the summer with your cousins."

"Me, too," was all Liz could manage to squeak out over the growing lump in her throat.

The two stared into each other's eyes and then Joshua surprised them both by saying, "I think I love you, Lizzie."

Liz froze at his words and then as natural as the sun shining after a cloudy day she stated shyly, "I think I love you, too."

Joshua then slowly, but deliberately lowered his face to hers and sealed the words with a long, lingering kiss.

As the kiss grew, so did their body heat and passion.

Involuntarily, Elizabeth's body moved even closer, but Joshua had other ideas.

Pulling back, but still with hands on her face, he said sadly, "I have to go, Lizzie. It's time."

Immediately the tears began flowing as Liz pleaded, "Not

yet, Josh! Please, not yet!"

With his thumbs, Joshua gently wiped her tears. "Sweetie . . . no time will be a good time and if I keep kissing you it will only make our parting that much more difficult. It has to happen so I think its best I go now. We'll each take with us the memory of our times together . . . and our kisses."

As she started to interrupt, Joshua's hand slid to her lips. "Lizzie, we have each other's phone numbers and I'll be calling. And always remember, anytime you need to talk and are able to call . . . please do . . . okay?"

Unable to speak over the pile of lumps now accumulated in her throat, Liz nodded as tears continued flowing.

Wiping them away one more time, Joshua leaned in to plant another warm kiss on her trembling lips and then dropped his hands to step back.

He started to walk away, but then changed his mind. Taking her back in his arms he pulled Liz close to his heart to whisper, "I don't think any more, Lizzie. I know that I love you!" Then without further warning, he briskly walked down the steps to his car.

Elizabeth put fingers over her still warm lips. As tears flowed down her cheeks, and off her chin, she whispered through her fingers, "I love you, too, Joshua. I love you, too."

When Joshua got to his car, he turned to raise one hand in a brief wave.

Elizabeth did the same and then he was gone.

She stared at the blank spot where his car had been and then went slowly inside. Almost immediately, her cousin walked up to ask, "Has he gone?"

Unable to reply, Liz raised tortured eyes her cousin's way and nodded her head.

Then, her cousin said something that broke Liz's heart even further.

"You need to keep a hold of that one! He's a keeper!"

Throwing her arms around her cousin, she wailed, "I don't know how! I'm going so far away! How do I keep him from forgetting me?"

Suddenly, Elizabeth stood straight with a peculiar look in her eyes and a wrinkle to her forehead.

Concerned, her cousin asked with a frown, "Are you all right? You look pale."

Elizabeth looked at her cousin and said in a dull voice, "I'm not sure what's wrong. My head started hurting and along with the pain came a kaleidoscope of pictures! They are playing rapidly over and over in my mind."

Her voice filled with wonder and yet a touch of fear as the head pain increased and so did the pictures.

The pain took Elizabeth's breath away leaving her unable to speak. Her mind soon became absorbed with the multitude of pictures floating around in her head; some of them too rapid to look at.

But others floated by her mind's eye slowly and Liz could clearly see her and Joshua's wedding picture; followed closely by a collage of baby pictures and children growing up.

Mixed in the pile were ones of her and Joshua in their twenties, then thirties, then forties, even fifties.

All of it was very bewildering, but the thing catching Elizabeth's attention the most was the head pain. Lowering her head to her hands, she felt like screaming when Elizabeth felt hands on her.

"Liz, Liz! What is it? What's wrong?"

In a strained voice, Elizabeth finally replied, "I have a bad headache and something . . . something . . . else . . . is . . . terribly . . . . wrong!"

With that . . . she grew limp and collapsed to the floor.

CHAPTER FIFTEEN

At 2:18 a.m. the night nurse urgently nudged Joshua Warner awake, jumpstarting him into a sitting position. Disoriented, it took a moment for him to remember where he was and why.

Right when Josh's mind filled with the accident events and Liz's injuries, the nurse began speaking effectively pushing Josh's already racing heart into a higher gear.

"Mr. Warner, CCU just called. They said we should bring you to see your wife, and for safety purposes we need you to go by wheelchair."

It took a few minutes for that conveyance to arrive, so Joshua was chomping at the bit by the time he arrived on the third floor twenty-three minutes later. The nurse picked up the receiver from the wall phone near the double CCU doors with Joshua impatiently awaiting the doors to be unlocked so he could be wheeled in to see what was wrong with his Lizzie.

But, once through the doors, Joshua didn't make it to Elizabeth's cubicle before the night doctor waylaid him.

"Mr. Warner, we need to talk."

The nurse immediately turned the wheelchair and moved it closer to the central nurse's monitoring station. Joshua's eyes darted toward Liz's room. He almost sighed with relief to see her there and that people weren't working over her.

Swinging his attention back to the doctor, he demanded, "What's going on? The nurse told us to come, but no one will tell me why."

"Mr. Warner, a few minutes before 2 a.m. your wife's vitals began showing stress. At first we thought it was related to your son's visit." Here the doctor paused to shoot a reproachful glare at one of the nearby nurses.

Joshua followed his look, but was confused. "My son? Was Tony here this early in the morning? And if so, why would you think it would cause her stress? As far as I know, she hasn't known when any of us have been here."

"Slow down, Mr. Warner . . . let me finish. As it turned out it had nothing to do with your son's visit." Now it was the doctor's turn to frown. "But, it wasn't your son Tony who was here. It was someone named Seth. Is he your son, too; or did we let a stranger in here?" Again he shot a narrowed look at the middle aged nurse.

At mention of Seth's name, Joshua froze. *Seth was here? When? How long?* He even took a moment to glance around the room as if he could still be there. As the questions whirled around in his head, Joshua mumbled, "He's our son but, we didn't . . . ."

His words broke off when a couple of people in surgical gear walked by into Liz's cubicle.

The doctor's eyes followed them and then he began talking more rapidly. "Mr. Warner, you're aware that head scans have been regularly done on your wife. Well, we did one at 2 a.m. The results revealed that her brain is swelling due to a blood hemorrhage just inside her skull above the left ear. Those results prompted me to have the nurse phone you. Your wife needs emergency surgery to help relieve the pressure before it becomes too great. I'll be honest with you Mr. Warner. If this is building quickly it could kill your wife. We need to move now."

"Emergency surgery! What are they going to do?" Joshua's eyes never left the activity going on around his beloved, as the questions came out.

"We have a brain surgeon getting ready as we speak. If it's some internal broken vessel caused by the accident trauma, all it should require will be a relatively small hole drilled in the vicinity of the swelling where the blood will be siphoned off." Most of that went into Josh's mind, but his attention was on the now leaving Elizabeth. As her gurney drew near, Joshua wheeled his chair forward with the intent of stalling their progress out the door. He needed to touch some part of her before they moved her out.

At the same moment, the doctor stopped him by taking hold of his good arm. "Mr. Warner, I can't stress the importance of speed here. You must not detain them."

The two surgery techs leveled eyes at him as she continued moving.

As it ended up all Joshua got was a brief feel of her toes as they hurried her out of the room.

He followed the disappearing group with his eyes, then turned back to stare with dismay into the now empty cubicle.

The doctor still standing beside him asked in a calm, but urgent voice, "Mr. Warner? Did you hear what I was telling you?"

Slowly focusing back on the doctor, Joshua nodded while asking, "And if that drilling procedure doesn't work? What then?"

"If the bleeding is caused from something else, that's another matter. They would then probably do a medically induced coma or possibly a newer procedure of cooling the brain down with ice. Both these procedures would slow the brain activity and let the brain rest."

To Joshua's chagrin the next question came out shaky and extremely tired sounding, "How long will the surgery take and where can I wait?"

"The nurse will direct you to the surgical waiting room. As to the length; you probably already know that depends on if the first procedure works or not. If it does . . . the surgeon should be out to speak with you in less than an hour."

The doctor started to say more, but right then the middle aged nurse walked up stating he was needed with another patient. At the same time, another nurse came over and Joshua shortly found himself sitting in an empty room waiting once again with his heart in his throat for word on Lizzie's current problem.

Unable to stay seated in the wheelchair, he wandered the room touching this and that, then came across a Gideon Bible. At the same moment thoughts of notifying his children swirled around in Joshua's mind. While staring blindly at the Bible laying in front of him, he considered his own frame of mind. Realizing he wasn't ready to deal with the added stress of anxious children, Joshua felt strongly that he needed to have a calmer spirit within himself. He needed private time with his Lord and His Word in order to better be the stabilizing force his children needed and would expect.

Having made his decision, instead of angling toward the nearby telephone, Joshua picked up the Bible. Holding it close to his heart with his good arm, he then walked to the nearest stuffed chair, sat down and wearily leaned his head back. He stared at the ceiling counting the tiles for a seemingly long time and then closed his eyes. He prayed fervently for the first surgery attempt to be successful and committed his Lizzie into the Lord's hands . . . once more.

Time sped by as Joshua's prayer grew less anxious and he became calmer. He knew God was in control and that no matter the outcome; Lizzie was in His hands . . . His very capable hands. A peaceful aura filled Joshua's heart and mind. He was so absorbed with God's warm presence that it startled him when the door suddenly opened. His eyes flew open to observe the surgeon walking in.

Minutes later the doctor walked back out and Joshua held a private praise service with the wonderful answer to prayer that the procedure had worked.

The bleed was caused by a couple of ruptured blood vessels which the doctor said they were able to take care of and that Lizzie was on her way to recovery.

Before exiting the room, the doctor added, "Your wife has a strong constitution, Mr. Warner. Once the pressure was taken care of, her vitals became quite stable, under the circumstances."

Even though Joshua was happy to hear the wonderful news, the bigger issue was that during his quiet time with the Lord he'd cleared away the barrier of distrust of his Lizzie in God's hands. Joshua realized how arrogant he'd been to think he could do a better job of caring for Lizzie then Jesus, and he remembered that she truly belonged to God . . . not him. *Nothing takes my Heavenly Father by surprise and nothing is too big for Him. If God wants Lizzie to come back to us, then that's what will happen.*

If He doesn't, well . . . as much as Joshua hated to think on it . . . he knew the Lord would give him the strength to deal with that, too.

Earlier before exiting the room, the doctor insisted Joshua head back upstairs to get more rest. "Your wife won't come out of recovery for at least an hour and then she'll be back in CCU. You'll do her better if you get the proper rest and then come back tomorrow morning."

Heeding the doctor's words, Joshua and his nurse went back to his room.

It wasn't until the next morning that he remembered the CCU doctor mentioning his son's visit and that he'd said his name wasn't Tony . . . but, Seth.

Shortly after that, Joshua was released and with the help of Jenny, moved his things to the assigned room at the hospitality house attached to the hospital.

CHAPTER SIXTEEN

(Somewhere in Time)

Elizabeth Warner was confused.

She didn't recognize anything of what she was seeing.

Another thing bothering her was the sense of fear coursing through her body and mind.

Okay, Liz, take it slow. Get your bearings. What do you see?

The voice in her head had a calming effect. So much so that Elizabeth felt herself relaxing. She realized that her first images of where she was were blurred; now her surroundings were coming into focus. She was surprised to see her Joshua sitting on a sofa talking to another man; but then she frowned.

Something was still wrong with the perspective of her view.

As Joshua's image became clearer, Elizabeth was startled to realize she wasn't on their level. Instead, she was gazing down on the two men. She could easily see Joshua's full head of bushy hair and wondered about running her hands through it. The thought caused her to almost chuckle, but she wasn't sure whether or not the men could hear her.

Glancing around, Elizabeth looked for the staircase she must be standing on or even a banister she was looking down on them from. But to her utter amazement, she wasn't on either.

The fact was . . . she wasn't on anything! Elizabeth was floating in the air above their heads!

What's going on? Am I dreaming? Then a terrifying thought hit her!

Am I dead?

Panic began creeping over her body as Elizabeth tried understanding what was happening to her. It was then the words of the men below became audible to her ears, capturing Liz's attention.

Concluding this had to be a dream, Elizabeth decided to play it out and see what was going on. It piqued her interest to see just how creative she could be in her dream, so reveling in the idea of the adventure in eavesdropping on Joshua, Elizabeth smiled while angling herself down . . . the better to hear their words.

"Joshua, you and Elizabeth have been attending church regularly for some time now. The reason I invited you here tonight was to see if you had any questions about God, Jesus Christ, or the Bible."

Liz watched Josh's face grow thoughtful as he paused before admitting, "Lately, I have been wondering about a few things."

"Like what?"

"Well, for one thing the whole issue of heaven and hell. I find it hard to reconcile a loving God with One who would willingly send people to a place called hell, or Hades. According to you, those people will be in torment for eternity. That's a very long, long time!"

Elizabeth watched his brows furrow. She was sure he was probably thinking what she was . . . about the fact that if hell was a true place they both had family members who openly rejected God and the Bible. That thought also meant if they died in that state, they would live the rest of their days in torment. Liz could understand Josh's doubt . . . that was a lot to swallow in regards to family members and friends.

As the other man began responding, Elizabeth zeroed in on his reply. The answer suddenly became very important.

Unnoticed previously by Liz, the man had a Bible setting on his lap which he now opened.

"I believe the Word of God teaches hell to be a real place,

but rather than taking my word for it, let's see what the Bible has to say." He flipped some pages and then read, "Psalm chapter 55 verse 15 says: *'Let death seize them; Let them go down alive into hell, for wickedness is in their dwellings and among them.'*

"These words were written by King David and he believed in a literal place called Sheol or hell, depending on your translation."

He then flipped more pages. "Proverbs chapter 27 verse 20 says: *'hell or sheol and destruction are never full; so the eyes of man are never satisfied.'* King Solomon was regarded as one of the wisest men to ever live and yet he wrote these words. He, too, believed in a literal place."

"But those are in the Old Testament, let's move to the New Testament too . . . let's see . . . here's one; in Matthew chapter 18 verse 9. Jesus Himself is talking and he brings up the topic of *'hell fire'*. Then in chapter 23 verse 33 He becomes real vocal about it to the hypocritical Pharisees."

The man handed Joshua the Bible, asking him to read the verse out loud.

Elizabeth's senses tingled as the familiar voice of her beloved read the scripture. *"Serpents, brood of vipers! How can you escape the condemnation of hell?"*

Elizabeth grew thoughtful over the vehemence of Christ's words toward the religious leaders of His day!

She watched Joshua hand the Bible back, then heard him

slowly comment, "I guess it makes sense. There's so much evil in this world, it somehow seems fitting that there would be a special place made just for the worst of them. But family members? Friends? As I've already stated, eternity is a long time to sentence people who aren't murderers, or drug pushers, or rapists!"

"Joshua, you must keep in mind that it's not God who sends people to hell. His desire is for all to be saved. Second Peter 3:9 - says: *'The Lord is not slack concerning His promise, as some count slackness, but is longsuffering toward us, not willing that any should perish but that all should come to repentance.'* And then there's always the most well-known verse in the Bible - John 3:16. Jesus doesn't want anyone to perish. People send themselves to hell by rejecting Christ and the sacrificial work He did on the cross."

He let Joshua mull that over a bit and then asked, "Joshua, if you died and stood before God what would you say if He asked why He should let you into His heaven?"

Elizabeth listened as the man clearly explained about the consequences of Adam's sin in the beginning of time and how everyone is spiritually separated from God. He then showed Joshua a picture from the back of his Bible of a great gulf fixed between man and a Holy God. He then brought forward another one with a cross stretched across the gap allowing a way for anyone to freely cross over.

This talk went on for quite a while.

Elizabeth tried paying attention but other voices began reaching her ears from around her. She looked but didn't see anyone.

Wondering what direction her dream was headed now, Elizabeth focused back on the two men below her.

It startled her to see Joshua down on his knees with the man beside him. Joshua was saying something about needing God's Son, Christ Jesus in his heart. She couldn't see his face, but it stressed Elizabeth to hear tears in her beloved's voice. She wanted to go to him, but something held her securely suspended in the air.

Then, Joshua stood and he smiled in a way she'd never seen before. His face shone with an unknown peace . . . almost holy in appearance.

As she continued watching trying to understand what had just happened, the two men happily hugged and shook hands. The man called Joshua his brother in Christ. In that moment, Elizabeth's being filled with an unknown joy and she too wanted to be a part of what was going on below her . . . when suddenly she heard a voice and her name spoken.

Elizabeth cocked her head, for the voice sounded very familiar.

It also sounded profoundly sad . . . but then it turned almost angry.

Suddenly . . . there wasn't just one familiar voice – but two.

Her body tensed as Liz strained to hear the voices more clearly.

All was quiet a moment and then clear as a bell she heard one voice say, "All you do is think of yourself and cause pain to others!"

Then the other voice said, "You're right I did those things, but I'm not the same person anymore."

As the voice cracked over the last words, with a blow realization hit Elizabeth as to whom the voices belonged to.

The first one was her eldest son, Anthony.

But, it was the second one that caused her heart to still and then race.

It was her long lost prodigal son, Seth!

With all her might Elizabeth tried to speak, but instead . . . the far off voices faded away; the scene below her with Joshua and the man disappeared.

All went black.

CHAPTER SEVENTEEN

Tony Warner sat beside his Mom's bed holding her hand. Normally his visit happened after supper, but today was different; Tony hadn't slept well and had experienced a strong need to see her first thing that morning.

Now as he stared at her, a feeling of helplessness threatened to break the thin thread of composure holding him together. Almost three days had gone by since his parent's accident. His mother had done well with the emergency surgery to release the blood built up in her brain; so much so that last night they'd moved her out of the highly monitored cubicle into a private room on the fifth floor.

When his dad had told the family, Tony's heart had leapt with joy. Over the phone he said, "That's great news, Dad; that means Mom's improving, right?"

There had been a noticeable pause and then his dad had explained, "Not really. She's over the critical stage, yes . . . but, so far your Mom isn't showing signs of waking. The doctor said they're going to back down her meds to see how she responds to more pain. They don't want her to suffer, but they need her to start showing responses to stimulus."

Tony had fretted about his mother's pain levels most of the night; to the point he was anxious to see if the experiment had worked. So in he walked at a couple minutes before 7 a.m. It was before visiting hours, but Tony headed straight to her new room without talking to anyone and was glad to see his mother alone – no nurses around.

He picked up her hand to give it a squeeze . . . hoping she'd show some form of response. He was disappointed her eyes didn't fly open with their familiar blue twinkle or feel her hand squeeze his. Tony's eyes scanned her for any signs of movement. For a moment his breath caught for he thought he saw her one leg twitch for a couple seconds. It had been so fleeting, he wasn't sure, but that fed his hope.

It was enough to prompt pulling his chair closer. Seating himself, Tony picked up his mother's left hand again in hopes of prompting the legs to twitch once more.

This time he saw nothing. After a few more minutes of

staring, Tony's mind traveled to something his father had told him a couple days earlier –Seth had been by to see their mother.

Part of Tony was glad Seth had finally showed up, but it upset him that as of yet, no one in the family had heard from his brother. Seth still wasn't returning any calls; not that Tony had tried, but he knew Dad and Jenny had repeatedly left messages – to no avail!

Typical . . . Tony thought for the hundredth time. *Seth always thinks about himself first . . . never about the family or what our needs may be!*

Tony never understood his younger brother. Setting aside his resentment over Seth's stealing of his parent's attention not only as a child but still as an adult . . . Tony stared at his mother while trying to figure out what had gone wrong with Seth. Had his parents given him too much attention? In Tony's book – they had.

As Tony contemplated that thought, a voice niggled his conscience. *What about you, Tony? Were you the older brother you were supposed to be for Seth? Did you try teaching him My ways?*

The sudden words in his head caused Tony to stiffen as words of defense rapidly crowded the questions from his mind. Not wanting to consider any fault of Seth's attitude and behavior laid at his door, Tony focused back on his mother.

Speaking out loud he said, "Hey, Mom . . . Tony here. Dad says you can hear me."

His voice trailed off as his mom lay motionless.

Then suddenly an overwhelming fear of losing his precious Mom assailed Tony's senses – opening a floodgate to the pocket of tears he'd not allowed himself to shed. They began rolling down Tony's face as he said, "Mom, why weren't you there for me? You spent so much time with Jenny and Seth! I know they were younger, but I needed you, too!"

Tony's voice cracked as his anguish over missed times with his mom flowed naturally into the canker sore of his younger brother.

As contemplation of Seth and all the injustices he felt over the years coursed through Tony's body and mind, he suddenly heard a creak behind him. Figuring it to be a nurse or maybe his father, Tony dashed the tears from his face as he came to a stand. Composing himself the best he could, Tony pasted a smile on as he slowly turned toward the door.

To his shock and surprise . . . it wasn't a nurse or his dad - it was Seth standing there!

~ ~ ~ ~ ~ ~ ~ ~ ~ ~

It had been almost fifty-four hours since Seth's clandestine visit to his Mom's bedside. After leaving the parking lot that morning, he'd fully intended to crash a few hours at a buddy's and then head out of town.

At least that had been his plan . . . but once rested Seth found himself reluctant to leave the area until he knew mom was out of danger. Judging by the unanswered calls he'd received on his cell phone over those hours, Seth figured the nurse must have informed the family of his presence.

Even though Seth was secure in his newly rededicated life to Jesus Christ, he was reluctant to broadcast it to his family. Jenny would have been okay . . . she always seemed to show love and mercy to him when Seth had misbehaved.

His father and brother were another matter. Seth had a feeling his brother, Tony, would be skeptical and Seth just wasn't mentally up to being put through the third degree . . . at least not yet. He still felt like a sailor who'd been out to sea a long time and was trying to find his land legs. The last thing he needed was a self-righteous older brother deliberately trying to tear apart Seth's newfound faith.

Now it was 7 a.m. in the morning and Seth was once again in the hospital parking lot. He'd chosen that time for two reasons – one was that Seth was quite certain there wasn't any chance of running into Tony. The other was because Seth had relented and called his sister Jenny the afternoon before. She said their dad tried to be at their mother's room around 8 a.m. each morning. So, because of that Seth's plan was to see his mom and be long gone before his dad's customary arrival time.

Unfortunately when he picked up the CCU phone twelve

minutes later, Seth was informed his mom had been moved to the fifth floor. Irritated with himself, Seth realized that might have been the purpose of his father's call late the night before. Hurrying back to the elevator, he punched the up button impatiently a couple times before it finally arrived and opened its doors.

Seth kept glancing at his watch to judge how much time he still had. Locating his Mom's private room was easy, but when Seth arrived at the partially open doorway, he was stunned to hear his brother's voice.

His first impulse was to turn around and make a hasty retreat; but the catch and pauses in Tony's words caught his attention, so Seth moved a little closer to listen. He couldn't hear Tony's words, but he did catch an occasional sob which tugged at Seth's heart. His brother was obviously struggling with his mother's condition. Seth strained to hear if anyone else were in the room, but all he heard was Tony's words and occasional sobs.

Fearing his mother was growing worse; Seth opened the door and stepped in. He paused to await Tony's acknowledgement, but he didn't move. Thinking Tony hadn't heard his entry; Seth softly closed the door and then turned around to find Tony rubbing tears from his face while staring at Seth in disbelief – disbelief that rapidly turned into obvious anger.

Seth stayed where he was near the door. He was waiting to see what his brother's next move would be; which didn't take long.

Stiffening, Tony took a couple steps toward Seth. "How long have you been eavesdropping at the door and what are you doing here, anyway?"

Tony's vehemence startled Seth. Taking a defensive posture, he narrowed his eyes. "I would think that would be obvious! I came to see Mom."

At his words, Tony straightened to his full height. "You have no place here! You've done enough damage to this family. I won't have you causing any more!"

Seth felt anger trying to rise up his throat at his brother's words, but instead of freely venting as he'd done in the past, Seth sent a prayer heavenward asking the Lord to help him talk to his brother; something he'd never learned to do.

During his younger years, all Seth wanted was to be near his older brother . . . but Tony wasn't interested. He constantly pushed him away or told Seth to stop being a pest and get lost. It didn't help matters on those occasions when their mom had made Tony play with Seth, for as soon as she'd walk away, Tony would do something mean as payback. As they grew older, Tony became more and more critical of Seth's behavior.

By the time Seth was in high school, Tony had graduated and was attending a Christian University to be a Youth Pastor. Seth had hoped that their relationship would get getter with time, but instead Tony began hounding Seth about all the things he did wrong

. . . which just added cold water to Seth's already struggling flame of faith. What Seth had wanted from his brother was acceptance and for Tony to lovingly show him how to live right.

But . . . Tony never had.

Now, with him once again pronouncing what a worthless son Seth was . . . something snapped inside Seth's head and he took a step forward while drawing himself to his full height; which was now equal to Tony's.

With a slightly raised voice he stated, "I have every right to be here. I'm as much her son as you are!"

Tony tensed and then took another step toward Seth. With his own voice now much louder he said, "You're no son to her. You haven't been for years! All you do is think of yourself and cause pain to others!"

Part of Tony's words struck home; which caused Seth to pause. He felt a sudden need to explain his changed life and with that need Seth's defensive posture melted away.

Cocking his head slightly, Seth stared past Tony to his mother to say in a soft voice, "You're right, Tony. I've not been a good son." Then swinging eyes back to his brother's Seth added, "But, I'm not the same person. Christ Jesus . . ."

Before Seth could finish his sentence Tony interrupted.

"Don't you dare try to sound all saintly and spiritual! You can't do what you've done and think it's erased by bringing Christ into it!"

Seth started attempting to explain once more about the marvelous change in his life when the door suddenly opened and a nurse marched in – a very agitated and commanding nurse.

"Do you men have any idea how loud you're being?" Not allowing time to reply, she went on to order them out of the room. "I don't know who you are and frankly I don't care! My responsibility is the care of this dear woman and I will not allow you to carry on like this in her vicinity!"

Immediately Seth grew embarrassed and ashamed.

But, Tony grew defensive, trying to blame Seth.

The nurse was in the process of interrupting his excuses when a bell on one of Elizabeth's machines went off.

In the following seconds . . . in walked Joshua Warner, followed closely by Jenny.

Within seconds of scanning the room, Joshua had a fairly good idea what had happened. Growing stern, he said, "Boys, step into the hallway. Wait for me there!"

Before turning toward Elizabeth and the nurse now taking her vitals, Joshua took a moment to touch Seth's arm. "Please, don't leave, son. I'll be out in a moment."

Joshua intended to stick near Elizabeth, but with the bell still going off, another nurse entered the room. Joshua and Jenny were then summarily ushered from the room.

Once back in the hall, they found Tony and Seth leaning against opposite walls not looking at each other. Making sure Elizabeth's door was firmly closed, Joshua turned to study his sons. While closing the door, both had pushed away from the wall and were staring at their father.

Joshua figured the brothers had been exchanging harsh, probably even loud words which had culminated in the speech he'd caught the tail end of from the nurse. Now, he contemplated how best to deal with the situation when Tony stepped close to give his version.

With a raised hand, Joshua stopped him. "Tony, this isn't the place. What say all of us go to the hospital café for something hot to drink and have a talk there?"

Getting a nod from his two sons, Joshua turned to lead the way with a bewildered Jenny at his side when the intercom crackled to life asking a doctor to immediately report to Elizabeth's room number.

The foursome retraced their steps. Within seconds they arrived back at Elizabeth's door; the same time the doctor did. They moved to follow him in when once again they were stopped from entering by the nurse. When asked what was going on, she stated, "The doctor will be out in a bit and you can speak with him then."

Joshua wiped a hand across his face, and then leaned against the wall near Elizabeth's door. Jenny soon joined him, but the brothers impatiently paced the hall while taking pains to avoid each other.

At one point, Seth paused to study his dad and sister to find them holding hands with heads bowed. He made a move to join them when the doctor stepped out. He eyed the little group and then signaled them to draw close.

Once all were near, he said with a scowl, "I understand there was an altercation in my patient's room a few minutes ago."

Seth lowered his head in silence at the implication in the doctor's voice. He heard Tony start to defend himself once again, but the doctor silenced him.

"Mr. Warner, as you know I ordered your wife's meds to be lowered. I was pleased to see she was doing so well; even to the point of moving her toes when they were stimulated."

Seth's head came up at his words and he noted Tony's raised eyebrows when the doctor told of their mom moving her toes. He wondered what that was about, but didn't have time to speculate for the doctor had stopped talking. Pulling his eyes from Tony's face to the doctor's, Seth was met by a pair of penetrating, accusing eyes. The doctor settled that look on both the boys before addressing Joshua again.

"Unfortunately, the angry voices of your sons appear to have stressed her. I've ordered the portable PET scanner to be brought up. Your wife's breathing has suddenly become more labored and

I need to see if more hemorrhaging is going on in her brain. If there is, I'm concerned your wife will slip into a coma."

He let that register a moment.

Joshua was stunned at the turn of events. "A coma? What does that mean?"

"I'm not sure yet. I'll know more after the scan."

Thoroughly rattled, Joshua stuttered, "If . . . if she goes into a coma . . . how long. . . I mean . . . how long would that last?"

"I've known some to last less than an hour, while others can last years."

With that he briefly laid a hand on Joshua's shoulder. "We'll keep you posted, Mr. Warner."

As the scanner came rattling down the hall, the doctor turned to Tony and Seth. "I've half a mind to band you both from your mother's room. What you did was inexcusable!" He furrowed his eyebrows to emphasize his point. After a long, hard stare the doctor walked to the nearest nurse's station.

Seth raised sorrowful eyes to his father and Jenny, and then turned toward his brother. He wanted to apologize, but Tony had other ideas.

Without a hint of embarrassment or shame evident on his face over his part of the argument, Tony stated, "Once again . . . look what you've caused!"

He then stalked away.

CHAPTER EIGHTEEN

When Tony stalked off, Jenny started after him but Joshua stopped her.

"I'll go. Stay here with Seth and wait for any possible update on your mother."

He then turned to fold Seth in a one armed hug. "I'm so glad you're here, son. Please don't run off. We need to talk."

"I won't, Dad . . . and I'm sorry about Mom. I never intended to cause any more hurt to this family."

"I know Seth. Don't take Tony's words to heart. We all have things God's trying to teach us . . . even Tony."

Joshua stared into his son's eyes a moment longer, and then turned his gaze to Jenny. Smiling he told them both he loved them and left to catch up with Tony.

Jenny stared at her father's back until it disappeared down the stairwell. Figuring her father thought that taking the stairs might get him to Tony faster, she turned to face Seth.

The two stared at each other a long moment, and then Jenny stated softly, "Wow! What an emotion packed few minutes!" She shook her mane of brunette hair as if to dispel the recent past from her memory and stepped forward to hug her brother. They held each other a long minute, then Jenny stepped back to better survey her younger, yet taller brother.

"You look good, Seth. Better than you did the last time I saw you. Your hair is shorter and it looks like you've put on a little weight."

Seth shrugged. "I've been taking better care of myself over the last few weeks – you know . . . eating better, less drinking and . . . other things."

Jenny glanced back at their mother's door before saying, "What say we get out of the hall and go talk?"

Seth too stared at the door before nodding his approval.

Before leaving the area, the two of them stopped at the nurse's station to ask if there was some way they could be paged if needed in regards to Elizabeth. Jenny was then handed a small pager with the words, "Sometimes we provide these for the families of critical patients. Just be sure to bring it here once you're back on the floor."

After assuring her they would and then asking the nurse to please let their father know they'd gone to the café, a short time later the two sat downstairs sipping hot chocolate frothed with whipped cream. For the first ten or fifteen minutes Jenny did most of the talking. She could see that Seth was deeply troubled; she could also see that something was different about his eyes. Over the last years it had saddened Jenny the amount of callousness and recklessness she'd observed in his face and demeanor.

But now . . . something was definitely different and it intrigued her.

Eventually, she got Seth to talk about what had happened between him and Tony. A couple times during the story, Jenny grew indignant at the cruel way Tony had spoken to Seth. Knowing in her heart that no one calling themselves a Christian should talk that way to another person . . . let alone her youth group leading brother, Jenny decided it was time to take the matter to her father.

Jenny's thoughts of Tony were curtailed when Seth said, "Jenny, the confrontation I had with Dad and Mom at my last visit disturbed me greatly. I left so angry and yet, deep in my heart I knew they were right."

As Seth went on to explain the spiritual war that had taken place in his heart and mind over the next few weeks, Jenny placed a comforting hand on his. It saddened her that he'd gone through so much. Life had gotten a hold of him and he had scars . . . not physical ones but emotional and even spiritual. She sighed for all the people trying to find their way in this possession obsessed do-your-own-thing-no-matter-how-it-hurts-others world.

Doing the inner city ministry, she often encountered the rebellious, angry attitudes of even young children struggling to understand the why's of poverty, senseless killings, aborted babies, homeless people, jobless people, and the list went on.

Jenny would prayerfully try guiding the ones in her contact to the saving knowledge of Jesus Christ . . . not as a good luck charm or that everything would be perfect . . . but as a way to help make sense of our world and what's happening in it.

When Seth came to the part where God sent a Bible-believing Christian across his path, Jenny's heart leaped for joy. Seth explained the impact this man had on his life and how it got him to thinking about his upbringing in general and the Word of God in particular.

"Jenny, he wasn't telling me anything new. Dad and Mom had done their jobs well. I knew the truth of God's Word, but for some reason a strong part of me yielded to the idea of rejecting it."

Seth stopped talking to stare blankly at the salt shaker on the table. "I've been such a fool, Jenny. I willingly walked right into satan's trap for my life!"

Swinging his eyes back to her lovely face, he asked, "Do you remember Dad's sermon about the Snare of the Fowler?"

"Sure . . . that particular sermon reminds me often to watch where I walk or what I do."

"Exactly! Dad stressed the fact that as a former trapper he had to study the habits of the animals he was after. That's what satan and his minions do with us."

Seth withdrew his hand still being held by hers and put his elbow on the table. Placing his chin in his hand, he continued. "We, human beings, are so arrogant! We think we're smarter than satan and the evils of this world . . . we're not!"

The two grew silent while contemplating the truth of Seth's words.

Then Jenny broke the silence. "Isn't it wonderful that Christ gives the victory? Satan thinks he's winning, but we've already won the fight! Christ Jesus took care of that at the Cross and then with His resurrection. It's what Easter's all about."

Again the two fell silent. Seth was mulling over how his life had changed lately, while Jenny was praying and hoping her brother would give her the good news that he was back in fellowship with his Savior again. She didn't realize she'd actually bowed her head slightly and closed her eyes until Seth spoke.

"Sis . . . are you praying?"

Jenny's eyes flew open as she smiled sheepishly. "Yes . . . in fact, I was praying for you, little brother; something I've done daily over the past few years."

Love and gratitude poured out Seth's eyes bathing Jenny in a warm glow.

"Thanks. That means more than you can possibly know. I knew Mom and Dad did and I figured you might be too, but it's always nice to know for sure."

Seth sighed deeply before saying, "All along the Holy Spirit kept nudging me and wooing me, but I'd deliberately ignore Him by doing something stupid and wild. My thinking was that eventually the Holy Spirit would leave me alone . . . He didn't. Then He brought a strong Bible believing man across my path and my attention was caught. I'd been ignoring the Holy Spirit's promptings so long that when I began honestly listening to the man's words and acknowledging my sins the peace that started seeping in was amazing!"

Seth sat up and then reached over to place his hand over his sister's. "In spite of all that . . . I still held back. Then, I got the message of the accident. Like a light going on in my head, everything changed. I knelt by my bed to ask Christ's forgiveness. I had to, Jenny! I wanted Him to hear my prayers for Mom and I wasn't sure He would until I got things right with Him."

By that time unheeded tears were rolling down both their faces. Seth's hand still lay over Jenny's which she topped with her own free one as he continued.

"Jenny, it was amazing! You know how people say they can literally feel burdens roll off their backs? That's exactly how it felt. Along with the lightness came a strong assurance of God's presence with me through the comfort of the Holy Spirit residing within me. I don't know how long I knelt there but when I stood I knew that Christ had never left me in the first place . . . I was the one who'd turned away – not Him. I also knew I had to see Mom for myself. And . . . here I am."

As he'd been speaking time had been rolling by and the two became slowly aware of what was happening around them. Squeezing each other's hands one last time, they then pulled away to mop their faces. Not finding a tissue in her purse, Jenny used a napkin from the table. She blew her nose before saying, "I'm so glad you came home. We all are."

"I wouldn't go that far. Tony made it pretty clear how he feels about my presence."

Jenny brushed that aside with a wave of her hand. "He will when he hears the wonderful news . . . besides, like Dad said . . . we all have spiritual growing to do. In some respects, I think that applies especially to our older brother."

The two talked a while longer about casual things before coming to a stand and leaving the nearly full café. Once out front, Jenny assumed Seth would go back upstairs with her, but he declined. He wasn't ready to chance seeing Tony again. Promising he wasn't leaving town and that he wouldn't avoid phone calls any more, the two hugged; then parted ways.

After returning the pager at the nurse's station, Jenny was disappointed to find her father alone in the hospital room. She'd fully expected to find Tony with him. After being told her mom's breathing was worse and that they'd upped the meds once more, Jenny tried getting her father to tell if he'd caught up with Tony and what had happened.

Not wanting to chance causing Elizabeth any more stress, Joshua pulled Jenny aside to whisper that he had indeed caught up with Tony and they'd talked.

By the expression on her father's face, Jenny was sure it hadn't gone well. She prodded for more details but Joshua firmly stated they'd talk later in his room and moved back to Elizabeth's side.

Curiosity was killing Jenny, but there wasn't anything she could do about it. Instead . . . having gotten permission from Seth to tell their father his good news, Jenny excitedly pulled a chair closer and did just that.

About an hour later, Jenny could see her father was tired so insisted he go rest while she stayed with her mom. After he left, Jenny faced the two chairs. Sitting in one, she placed her shoeless feet in the other, pulled out a book and began reading.

Sometime later, a nurse startled her awake. Embarrassed

that she'd fallen asleep, Jenny swung her feet down and sat up. She watched the nurse checking Elizabeth's monitors and then quietly asked, "How's she doing?"

The nurse finished checking the vitals before turning to answer Jenny. "As you can see, your mother's breathing is becoming shallower and more labored."

While the nurse was talking, Jenny kept glancing at her mom. The struggle to breath was definitely getting worse.

"What can be done to help her?"

"The doctor has ordered a ventilator to be inserted."

Seeing Jenny's stricken look, the nurse said, "I'm sorry, sweetie. I know this isn't easy on the family, or her." The nurse stared at the patient. "It is a setback but she can still recover. Many times ventilators are just a temporary measure to make breathing more normal for the patient."

Before leaving the room, the nurse stated, "You're father has already been notified about the ventilator. I believe he'll be headed here shortly."

Jenny smiled and said, "Thank you," then focused back on her mom.

Gently lifting her warm yet very still hand, Jenny prayed for her precious mother. While doing so, memories of the two of them singing duets together came strongly to Jenny's mind. Finished with the prayer, Jenny found herself humming one in particular. Deciding her mom might need to hear it, she pulled up the chair so she could sing nearer her mother's ear.

"Every day they pass me by, I can see it in their eyes.
Empty people filled with cares, heading who knows where.
On they go through private pain, living fear to fear.
Laughter hides their silent cries, only Jesus hears.
People need the Lord, people need the Lord,
At the end of broken dreams, He's the open door.
People need the Lord, people need the Lord,
When will we realize - people need the Lord.

As the song progressed, it became harder and harder for Jenny to sing. Finally giving up altogether, Jenny whispered, "I'm sorry, Mom."

She then laid her cheek on her mother's shoulder and cried.

CHAPTER NINETEEN

By the time Tony got back to his desk at the church, he was considerably calmer. Upon catching up with him, Tony's dad had wanted to sit down somewhere in the hospital and talk, but all Tony wanted to do was get as far away from Seth as he could. Joshua had tried to talk him out of leaving, but Tony had his mind made up, so in the end his father had relented and walked beside him out to the car. He'd tried to understand why Tony was so upset with his younger brother. Tony knew in his dad's mind all of them should be rejoicing at his brother's appearance.

Tony plopped in the chair behind his desk and wearily placed his face in his hands while stating bitterly to the air, "You don't understand, Dad. You never have."

He groaned at the turmoil broiling around in his insides. Part of Tony knew his response hadn't been godly where Seth was concerned; but, Tony was hurting so much in regards to his mother's condition and Seth was an easy target for his pent up emotions.

"Besides," Tony reasoned out loud. "Someone needs to let Seth know how it really is and how much he's hurt all of us."

Now, Tony believed Seth had a pretty clear picture.

"Then why do I feel so crappy about the whole thing?" Tony groaned into his hands.

Sitting back in his chair, Tony rubbed his face while remembering his dad's words. He'd listened patiently to Tony's ranting all the way to the car. Once there, his dad placed a firm hand on his shoulder to say, "You know, Son….at this moment I could be very angry with both you boys for the possible setback you've caused your mother. I could remind you the number of times I've told you that even though she's heavily medicated the hearing still works."

At that point, his dad's voice had choked and Tony's heart had lurched for the first time at the chaos he and Seth had created.

Joshua cleared his throat to go on to say, "But what good would all that blame do? The damage is done – its history – and bitter words just lead to more hurt."

He had then paused waiting for Tony's eyes to meet his.

"Son, if we're going to deal with this situation properly and endure the long haul of recuperation that lies before us, we have to pull together as a family – for your mother's sake and for our sake."

His father pleaded with Tony to get beyond whatever was bothering him about Seth . . . "forgive him and let's love him back to Christ. Don't you think that's what Jesus would have us do?"

Tony knew he stiffened at the words of his father, and now he said again to the air, "It's not that simple, Dad. Seth has been a sore in my flesh for too long."

Part of Tony wanted to be free of the anger he harbored toward his brother, and that part of him directed Tony's eyes to the Bible beckoning him from the corner of the desk. It was then he recalled his father's parting words as Tony had reached for the car door handle.

"Son, you have a wonderful ministry opportunity before you dealing with the youth of your church, but you're not going to be truly effective until you deal with this lack of forgiveness and hardness toward Seth. You may not believe that . . . but I'm telling you a truth. Jesus says we can't love others to Him if we don't love our brothers. That applies to the taking of communion, too. You're not to participate if you have something against your brother or they against you."

During this lecture Tony had tried presenting his side several times, but his dad had ignored him. Finally having enough, Tony declared, "I need to go," and opened his car door to emphasize the point.

He felt his father's eyes upon him but Tony refused to look back. Starting the engine, he heard his dad say, "Son, I'll be praying for you. Our black sheep, prodigal son has returned home. We should be throwing a feast . . . not trying to drive him away again."

Tony's eyes fell on the Bible where the story of the prodigal son's return beckoned him to read the account again in the New Testament Book of Luke, chapter 15. So much so, that Tony leaned forward to pull his Bible closer when a knock sounded at the partially open door and a head popped in.

"Hey, Mr. Tony. Got a sec?"

Tony stared with surprise at the young black teenager walking in.

"Hi, Booker, haven't seen you in a while. What gives?" Tony asked while pushing up from his desk and walking around to the front. He extended his hand for a shake, then indicated for Booker to take a seat in the nearest overstuffed chair.

As he did, Tony scooted one hip on the front of his desk, folded his arms and stated, "It's good to see you. I haven't seen you in youth group for a long while."

When Booker flopped into the chair he did it at an angle with one arm draped over the back and a leg over the arm of the chair.

Briefly Tony considered telling him to sit properly but this troubled youth from a local gang had been greatly in his prayers. Now that he'd willingly paid Tony a visit, he didn't want to do anything to hinder his returning. Curious as to why he'd come, Tony asked, "Is something on your mind?"

Before answering, Booker deliberately scanned the room with raised eyebrows at the quality furniture and desk items he was looking at. His mind considered what value they'd bring on the street, before shaking the image away and bringing his eyes back to the youth pastor.

"Yah, I've got something on my mind. You see . . . my aunt, who's an aide at the hospital, stopped by to see ma. Me having a late night and crashing at ma's, wandered into the kitchen an heard her telling of an argument that happened in a patient's room this morn."

As Booker talked his eyes narrowed and Tony felt his body tense. *Surely, he wasn't about to talk about . . .*

Booker continued. "These two men were so loud the nurses and auntie could hear them down the hall." Narrowing his eyes, Booker added, "Actually, auntie said one man in particular was the loudest."

Panic began surging in Tony's gut as he saw where the story was headed; Tony forced himself to appear calm . . . waiting for the punch line.

"The thing is, Mr. Tony," Here Booker stared at the

fingernails of his left hand before raising dark eyes Tony's way. "The thing is . . . auntie swears that loud, angry man was you, Mr. Tony. And she says you was talking real mean to the other man. When I heard that, I says to her face that she must be wrong. We got into it cuz she says I called her a liar. Ma finally told me to come ask you."

Here he paused a long moment . . . all the while studying Tony's face. Whatever he saw bothered Booker greatly because a deep frown creased his brow as he swung his draped arm forward to point accusingly at Tony.

"It was you, wasn't it, Mr. Tony? I sees it all over your face!"

Tony came to his feet. "You don't know the whole story, Booker. Let me . . ."

But Booker jerked his leg down to sit straighter and then interrupted with, "Who was he, Mr. Tony? Who was the other man?"

Taking a deep breath Tony admitted, "It was my younger brother." He then hurried on to say, "You don't know the pain and grief he's caused my family. You don't . . ."

Again Booker cut him off.

"Hold on man! I'm not stupid! I get what you're laying down, man! Your bro's not a good Christian man like you . . . right? I mean . . . he's not a saint like you, right?" Tony started to reply, but Booker's words penetrated and he paused to consider. *Is that the way I think about Seth? Deep down do I think I'm better than him because I'm the good son and he's not?*

The thoughts reeled him, but a thoroughly roused Booker wasn't done.

"If your own brother isn't good enough then where does that leave me? You know, man, I was beginning to buy your words about God and my need of Him and how it would be good for me. Are you feelin me, man?"

For the life of him, Tony couldn't think of a response. He felt like a condemned man before a judge. Fear coursed through at the thought of losing this young man all because Tony had given in to his flesh and allowed his bitterness to be witnessed by people at the hospital and now . . . it was affecting Booker. Who was now staring at Tony with bitterness and disappointment written all over his young face.

"I member your talk the last time I was at youth meetin, it was on forgiveness and love. You said unforgiveness was like a cancer. It ate us from the inside out. You said that God was the divine healer. You said He could take it all away and make us clean inside. You also said everyone is equal in God's eyes, that He forgives all who come to Him."

Every time Booker used the words – you said – Tony flinched. Each one was a direct hit to his heart and his conscience.

"Now I see it's all a lie! You're the one full of cancer! Do you even believe the words in that book?" As Tony rose to his feet, a condemning finger pointed at the Bible lying on Tony's desk. "Everythin you said was crap! Pure crap! So . . . who needs it?"

Booker shot one final angry look at Tony and then left the room . . . slamming the door behind him.

Thoroughly shaken, Tony stared at the closed door a long, long time before making his way back around the desk.

Collapsing into the chair, he laid his forehead on the desk and wept.

"Lord Jesus, what have I done? What have I done?"

CHAPTER TWENTY

"Mom, everything's such a mess!"

Jenny laid her cheek on her mother's hand.

Another day had passed since the boys had their run-in and in spite of the ventilator being installed, her mom's vitals were still worsening.

The evening before, Seth had a long talk alone with their father. He'd asked his forgiveness for all he'd done in the past and for his involvement with their mother's worsened condition. After the two had prayed and cried together, they'd walked to Elizabeth's room and Seth had asked Jenny's forgiveness, too.

Over the next hour the three of them quietly chatted while seated around Elizabeth's bed waiting for Tony's appearance. Other than his unexpected visit early the morning before, Tony's usual time to visit was in the vicinity of 8 p.m.

As the trio waited, the time came and went without Tony showing up.

At 8:15 p.m., Jenny called his cell phone which went immediately to voicemail. With concern written all over her face Jenny stated, "Tony's cell phone is shut off."

When he hadn't shown up by 9 p.m. the three of them kissed Elizabeth good bye and headed out; Joshua to the hospitality house, and the other two to their old bedrooms at their parent's home.

At lunch the next day in the hospital cafeteria, Seth voiced his concern that Tony might be staying away because of his presence; and then stated he thought it was time the two had a face to face talk. Rising to his feet, Seth stated he was going to find his brother.

To which Joshua replied, "Seth, I'd like to come with you. I believe in my heart it needs to be both of us. Let's start at the church. I expect he'll be there. It's a good place to talk without interruptions."

"And if he's not there?" Seth asked.

"Then, we'll try his apartment and then his girlfriend's cell phone."

Joshua stepped closer to his youngest son. Placing a hand on his shoulder he said, "We'll find him and this rift between the two of you will be dealt with once and for all."

That had been four hours earlier and as of the last call, the two still hadn't found Tony in any of the places mentioned.

Jenny was becoming quite worried. *Where could he be?*

She sat up to stare at her mother. The ventilator tube down her throat and ample amounts of tape covered up most of her lower face. The doctor had told the family that Elizabeth's brainwaves were slowing and with it her natural ability to breathe on her own; for now the machine was breathing for her.

As Jenny stared at her precious mom's face, she could see more prominent cheek bone structure. She also observed that the eyes had stopped moving. She doubted her mom was dreaming any longer.

Not wanting to dwell on her mother's slowly failing condition; Jenny forced her mind to other things . . . mainly Scott Holland.

She'd met him a few months back and since then they'd had several dates. Most of the time they were with other singles from the church she attended; but lately they'd found themselves doing things separate from the group.

Jenny hadn't mentioned him to her parents for she originally didn't think anything would come of it. Her first love was Jesus Christ and she was committed to serving Him with the inner city ministry.

The last couple of weeks things between her and Scott had begun to change. He had started dropping in unannounced at Jenny's mission looking for her and leaving more personal messages on her cell phone. She wasn't sure how to feel about all his attention, but did have to admit that she was beginning to think about him more and more, which caused a conflict in her soul.

As these thoughts roamed in her mind, Jenny found herself needing to tell it all to her mom – her closest friend. So over the next half hour she did just that. Jenny started by sharing about their first date and things they'd done together since then. From there she moved on to how he made her feel as a woman when they were together.

She paused in her narrative to sigh in frustration, before stating, "Mom, the more I like being with him the more I feel I'm being disloyal to my calling from the Lord to be an inner city missionary. How can I allow myself to care for Scott? He works for a large law firm in the city and feels that's what God has called him to do. Normally, we never would have met, but Scott was helping his cousin who volunteers at a teen center where I do an occasional Bible study. Of course, I already knew Peter, but when I laid eyes on the man with him I thought he was one of the most gorgeous men I'd ever seen!"

Moving up to lay her head on her mom's good shoulder Jenny said, "Oh, mom . . . I don't know what to do with my growing feelings for Scott. I wish you'd wake up and tell me what to do."

Jenny jumped when a moment later the gentle hand of her father was placed on her shoulder.

"Sweetheart, I heard your words about Scott and your struggles with feelings for him. I know you'd prefer talking to your mother about this but under the circumstances . . . will I do?"

Jenny quickly rose to hug him. With tears she replied, "Of course you will."

While the two hugged, Seth walked in with three steaming lidded cups saying, "Two hot chocolates and one coffee with cream."

His lips smiled, but Jenny noticed his eyes were grave. She asked over her dad's shoulder, "Still no Tony?"

Seth bit his lip and shook his head.

She pulled away from her father, took the chocolate from Seth, and then turned back to her Dad. "Where could he be?"

"We haven't a clue," Joshua responded in a tired voice while retrieving his coffee.

Seth took a sip from his chocolate before adding, "We checked everywhere. His girlfriend hasn't spoken to him since the night before last. But, she didn't seem concerned. She said Tony often got tied up with some teen crisis or another and that she didn't usually hear from him every day."

"And, what about his church?"

"The Pastor said they spoke at noon yesterday. Tony was headed out the door as he was entering. The Pastor said his eyes were red and he looked distraught. Since he figured it had to do with Mom, when Tony asked for some days off he readily agreed. That's all we know."

Not having any more to say, Seth walked to his mom's side and quietly sipped his hot chocolate. He stared at her a long moment before saying, "Why don't you two take a break. I'll stay with Mom awhile."

Not feeling like being around others, Jenny suggested they go to their Dad's room, take their shoes off and talk.

Agreeing, Joshua assured Seth they'd be back in a couple hours.

Back at the hospitality house room, the shoes came off and drinks were reheated in the microwave. Joshua then pulled two chairs close together so they could prop their feet on the bed. Once they were both settled, he said, "Okay, kiddo, now tell me about your Scott and what the problem is."

About half an hour later, Jenny finished her saga with the lament, "Do I stop seeing him, Dad? What do I do? Am I being disloyal to the Lord?"

Joshua stared at the painting above the queen size bed before focusing back on his daughter.

"First of all, I don't think it's a case of disloyalty . . . I think

"Good morning, sweetheart. It's another glorious new day. One we're waiting to share with you." Pulling a chair close, he continued chatting while bringing her up-to-date on their three children.

After a while he ran out of things to say and his voice trailed off. Spying a Gideon Bible lying nearby, he decided to read her some scripture. Knowing the book of Philippians was one of Liz's favorite, he lowered the bedside tray as low as he could to better have access to the Bible with his one good hand. Joshua then turned to the New Testament and began reading at Chapter One.

"Paul and Timothy, bondservants of Jesus Christ, to all the saints in Christ Jesus who are in Philippi, with the bishops and deacons. Grace to you and peace from God our Father and the Lord Jesus Christ. I thank my God upon every remembrance of you…"

On and on he read. He paused a couple times to take long drinks from the bottle of water he'd purchased enroute to her room and once more when a nurse came in to check vitals. She silently did her job, nodded with sympathy and then walked from the room.

Joshua stared at her retreating back . . . then read on.

As he got to Chapter Four verses 4 – 7, his voice slowed. *"Rejoice in the Lord always, Again I will say rejoice! Let your gentleness be known to all men. The Lord is at hand. Be anxious for nothing, but in everything by prayer and supplication, with thanksgiving, let your requests be made known to God."*

His voice faltered at the next words.

"And the peace of God, which surpasses all understanding, will guard your hearts and minds through Christ Jesus."

Feeling a conflict arise in his heart over his lack of peace over Liz's latest plight, Joshua slowly closed the Bible to gently set it back on the stand. Leaning forward he lifted the blanket edge up to better hold her unmoving, smaller hand in his.

It was warm, but still non-responsive.

As he sat there staring at his beloved's pale face, his mind went back to their first meeting and consequent dates. Softly, he began speaking to her.

"Lizzie, do you remember our first dates? Of course you do; probably better than me. We had such fun, didn't we? You were concerned about our age difference, but six years was no big deal to me."

Here he chuckled while squeezing her hand, "Although during those first two months, at times it was pretty obvious you were only seventeen."

"Don't get me wrong, Lizzie. You were cute and adorable."

Then his voice grew serious. "I knew even then you were the one for me. Those months went by fast and before I knew it, it was time for me to return to the university in Louisiana."

Joshua paused to run his thumb over her hand. "Just think, Lizzie, if I hadn't taken a semester off to visit my parents in

Michigan and hadn't been invited to your sister's wedding . . . we'd have never met. I'm so thankful I came to that wedding all those many years ago! It changed the direction of both our lives."

He stood to plant a kiss on her nose and run his fingers through her bangs. Joshua studied her face a long time, then leaned close to her ear to state softly, "I love you, Lizzie. Please come back to me."

Tears threatened to choke him, so Joshua straightened to take his seat. Capturing her hand once more, he went on....

"I wanted you to come with me to Louisiana, but each time I asked, you grew indignant. It wasn't until much later that I discovered the reason. You thought I was asking you to come live with me."

Joshua chuckled over the thought, but then he frowned and rubbed her hand more intensely. "Driving away from your parent's home that last night was one of the hardest things I'd ever done. You stood crying in the driveway. I kept telling you I loved you and we'd be together again, but you looked like you didn't believe me. You looked so sad and fearful as I drove away. You told me later that you'd stood there a long time crying, then walked into the house. Your Aunt and Uncle were visiting that week from another state. You said your Aunt walked up and told you to keep a hold of me. It saddened me so when you told me you fell into her arms crying, "I don't know how!"

"Oh, Lizzie. You needn't have worried. You were the one, and only one for me. I'm sorry you hadn't understood that. Just like when you thought I was asking you to live with me. I admit . . . I did a poor job of asking you to marry me . . . then . . . but five months later, I did a much better job."

He reminded her of his decision to come to Michigan for a visit over Christmas and the two of them had sat along a back road one evening when he'd popped the question. Trying to sound indignant, he asked, "Do you remember your response? You laughed! Yes . . . you did! Well, actually I guess it was more a nervous giggle, but just the same!"

Sighing, Joshua squeezed her hand. "Oh, Lizzie, you had such a poor self-image. You couldn't believe anyone could love you enough to want to spend the rest of their life with you. But . . . you were wrong! I did . . . and still do."

A long silence filled the room as Josh studied the face of his beloved, before saying close to her ear, "Lizzie, I uncovered the Chevelle SS and started her up. She purred like a kitten. Actually, you know better, huh? She's no kitten, but she does have a nice rumble that's like music to my ears. Remember the fun times we've had taking her out and pretending we were dating again?" As memories flooded Joshua's mind, he chuckled. "We even went a few times to the popular making out place and did some kissing. Remember?"

Suddenly, a feeling of hopelessness threatened to overwhelm Joshua as he stared at Liz's unmoving body. Leaning forward, he kissed her hand, and then rasped, "Come back to me, Lizzie. I need you! I want to feel your sweet kisses again."

Raising tearstained eyes to the unseen sky, Joshua pleaded, "Lord Jesus, please! Thirty-four years hasn't been enough time with my Lizzie!"

From his pocket, Joshua pulled the photo found in Liz's hand after the accident. He studied it a long time, and then laying his head on the bed near her body, his shoulders shook with great sobs.

At that moment, unseen by Joshua, Liz's eyes twitched back and forth . . . one, two, three times . . . and then lay still once more.

~ ~ ~ ~ ~ ~ ~ ~ ~ ~ ~

The next evening the main topic of discussion was Tony's continued absence and his whereabouts. It wasn't like him and Joshua was beginning to wonder if foul play were involved. He, Jenny and Seth had just stepped away from Elizabeth's bed to discuss whether or not they should contact the police - when Tony suddenly appeared.

As one, the three turned to stare in surprise at his sudden appearance. But before they could say anything, Tony forestalled them with a raised hand; then beckoned them closer to the door away from his mother.

"Before anyone speaks, I have something I need to say."

He proceeded to tell them about Booker's visit the morning of his and Seth's argument. He also told them how spiritually devastated he was after Booker left.

"All I could think of was running. I wanted to get away from myself . . . which we all know is impossible. It was crushing me to think my actions could have put a permanent wedge between Booker and the Lord. I headed out the door not sure where I was going, when I encountered the Pastor. Not wanting to chit-chat, I requested some time off and was on my way."

Realizing his speech could take longer than anticipated; Tony paused and then asked if the four of them could finish talking in his father's room.

Joshua told his kids to go on, that he'd catch up. He wanted a moment to say good night to Lizzie. He joined them a few minutes later at the entrance to the guest house.

Once inside the room, Jenny and Seth shed their shoes to get comfortable on the bed while Tony and Joshua took the chairs.

Tony could tell all of them were bursting with questions, so he immediately went on with his story.

"I got in my car and then just sat there. I didn't know where to go or what to do. Then I remembered one of the teens telling about spending time in the summer at his grandfather's small cottage on a lake. I drove to my apartment to call for the grandfather's phone number. He was more than happy to let me use the cottage, so I packed a bag and drove there."

"The cottage was a one-room A-frame with a small indoor toilet and shower stall. He assured me there was food in the cupboards but no television or radio. That was fine with me. At that point the last thing I wanted was outside distractions. In fact, I even turned off my cell phone. The cottage was perfect for my need of no disturbance or clutter. I hadn't even grabbed the most important thing – my Bible. I just wanted thinking time . . . alone. I guess in my troubled mind I even thought that meant from God."

Here Tony paused to smile as he took a moment to look each of his family members in the eyes. He lingered a moment on Seth before looking down at his clasped hands to continue on with the narrative.

"In my hurry, I hadn't factored God into the situation. I already mentioned not bringing along my Bible; but of all things . . . a Bible was the first thing my eyes landed on when I entered the cottage. The other thing I noticed was that the room was brimming with reminders of Christ's presence; verses were posted everywhere! And the one that pestered me the most was Hebrews 4:12 – '*For the Word of God is living and powerful, and sharper than any two-edged sword, piercing even to the division of soul and spirit, and of joints and marrow, and is a discerner of the thoughts and intents of the heart.*'"

"Throughout that afternoon and through the entire next day

that verse was what my mind, heart, and soul dwelt on. What were the true thoughts and intents of my heart? I must have asked myself that question dozens of times! And I'll tell you . . . I didn't like what I was seeing and realizing about myself!"

With tears, Tony raised his head to look straight at Seth. "I finally got so sick of myself, I turned to the One I should have surrendered all this to years ago. Falling to my knees in front of the sofa, I begged the Lord Jesus to forgive my arrogant pride and to give me a chance to make things right with everyone . . . especially two people."

Tony wiped tears from his cheeks with his sleeve as he felt his dad's comforting hand squeeze his shoulder. Turning towards him, he said, "This morning, I began my search for Booker, but couldn't find him. At noon, I even went to his mother's apartment. My heart jumped into my throat when she informed me he hadn't been home since the morning Booker had the run-in with his aunt about me."

"As I left that dingy, dirty apartment, I begged the Lord to help me find him so I could make things right . . . before Booker did something really stupid. I just hoped he already hadn't!"

Once again Tony stopped his story to smile; only it wasn't directed at any of them. His eyes were focused on some pleasant scene in his own mind.

In a voice full of marvel, he said, "Then it came to me . . .

try the hospital chapel. It had come so out-of-the-blue that I tried pushing it away, but the thought persisted. Along with it came an almost forgotten memory of a vulnerable, sad Booker sharing with me a rare confession. When visiting his mom at the hospital one day, he'd wandered the halls and walked past the chapel. Curious, he'd opened the door to peek inside. What he saw drew him, but Booker said he'd felt unworthy to go in. Strangely the peacefulness of the room called to his troubled soul, so Booker told me he'd glanced around to see if anyone was looking, and then had quickly slipped in. Booker said he hadn't anticipated the safety and peace he'd felt once inside. He didn't stay long that first time, but Booker told me he'd gone back every time he felt overwhelmed by life's temptations."

With wonder in his eyes, Tony shook his head as he admitted, "That's where I found him . . . right here in the hospital chapel. The moment I walked in he tried to leave, but I stopped him by saying how sorry I was for not being the person I should have been and also for letting him down. As we were the only ones in the peaceful haven, the two of us sat down and had a really nice heart-to-heart talk. When we parted, Booker promised he'd come back to the youth group meetings."

Tony stopped to take a deep breath. As he slowly exhaled, his eyes landed on Seth.

"The Lord had answered my first petition of finding and

talking to Booker. Now, it's time for my second request...."

Before he could say anything more, Joshua came to his feet. "Jenny, get your shoes on. I think it's a good time for us to take a walk."

The two went to the hospital café. During their time there Jenny shared with her father the decision she'd come to regarding Scott Holland.

"Dad, since talking with you, I've done a lot of talking to the Lord and have come to a decision. At this time, I'm not really prepared to remain single all the rest of my days here on earth – even though I realize that could be what the Lord requires of me. Someday I would like a man in my life to love and cherish me like you do Mom; having said that, I'm also not ready to walk away from the inner city ministry quite yet. I honestly took out my feelings for Scott and realized I've been swayed by the attention of a handsome man. Don't get me wrong . . . he loves the Lord, but I've come to the conclusion that if I really felt true love for him I wouldn't be having this dilemma. I think that if he were the right man God intended for me, I'd be willing to follow him anywhere. What I mean to say is . . . I don't believe I'd be struggling with the issue like I am. I'd be like Ruth was in the Old Testament Book of Ruth."

Jenny raised one eyebrow at her father before going on to say, "If you'll allow me to paraphrase . . . it would go something like this – his people would be my people, his God would be my God."

With peace and calm radiating from her lovely face, Jenny added, "Once I get back home I'm going to break it off with Scott and focus my energies more diligently on the ministry."

She paused a moment and then added with an impish gleam in her eye, "Until such time as the guy of God's choosing comes along, would you consider still being the special man of my life?"

"Since the day of your birth I have been and always will be," he promised with a warm answering smile.

~ ~ ~ ~ ~ ~ ~ ~ ~ ~

When Joshua and Jenny returned to the room an hour and a half later, they rejoiced to see the obvious change between the two brothers. They never heard all the details of what had transpired, but enough to know that something magnificent and Godly had taken place.

A big part of Joshua rejoiced over everything that had recently transpired, but then as always . . . Joshua's mind traveled to his beloved Elizabeth. He knew she'd been praying for years that the two boys would overcome their differences and become good friends. It pleased him to see that it looked like her prayers were being answered.

Now, Joshua hoped and prayed that she'd return to them so they could share all the good news with her.

CHAPTER TWENTY-TWO

Days crept by with no change in Elizabeth Warner.

At the one week mark, Joshua decided to give up the room in the hospitality house to move back home. Liz's condition weighed extremely heavy on him and evening time spent alone wasn't helping his frame of mind. It comforted Joshua to be home with Jenny and Seth, and to have morning prayer times together before he headed to the hospital.

By the end of one and one half weeks, Joshua and his children had fallen into a routine. Joshua was at Lizzie's side first thing each morning. Jenny took his place at noon so Joshua could get back to doing ministry calls with people of his congregation. Seth usually showed up between 3 and 4 p.m. And since Tony lived in the area and had his youth ministry job, he'd pop in whenever convenient during the day. Then, the four of them would gather after supper and stay until visiting hours were over at 9 p.m.

Every morning, Joshua and the doctor would talk. Each time he was told the same thing – "there's no change." Joshua would then ask if the doctor thought Elizabeth would and could still wake up. To which the doctor would patiently say that Liz could wake up that day or go on like this for weeks or even months.

Because of his consistent words, Joshua began entertaining the idea that Jenny and Seth should start getting on with their lives; Jenny back to her inner city ministry and Seth, to find a job wherever it was he felt God was leading him.

The problem was . . . Joshua still wasn't ready to acknowledge or admit that Elizabeth's condition could be a long term one. He fervently prayed the Lord would have her wake up and join them back in this world.

At the two week mark since the tragic accident, Joshua walked into Elizabeth's room as usual, only this time the doctor said that a change had occurred during the night.

Hope surged in Joshua as his eyes quickly darted to his Lizzie, but then he frowned at what he saw there; she looked the same as always.

Not understanding what the doctor meant, Joshua turned to question him when the doctor spoke up, "Mr. Warner, I'm sorry to get your hopes up, but it's not a good change. Tests show that your wife's vitals and brainwaves have taken a noticeable drop."

The doctor's announcement sent Joshua's heart jumping into his throat and then plummeting down into the pit of his stomach – leaving a queasy, sick feeling. Gathering his thoughts, Joshua asked if that meant Liz was dying.

As before, the doctor wouldn't commit himself, except to say – "not necessarily. She still could exist a long time in this state, especially with the ventilator keeping things going."

For the first time Joshua's senses zeroed in on the machine helping Liz breathe. Was it really doing more than that? Was the machine the only thing keeping her alive? As those questions attacked his mind, a new fear assailed his heart – a fear that sometime he could be asked permission to shut the thing off!

Forcing his mind away from that horrible thought, Joshua focused on the doctor's next words.

"Over the next days you and your family need to begin looking for a long term facility. Your insurance coverage for the hospital is running out and if your wife stays the way she is, she'll need to be moved."

The doctor's dismal words stayed with Joshua long after he left the room; so much so that as Jenny's usual arrival time drew near, Joshua decided he needed time alone to think and pray. He needed time to formulate some workable plans before talking seriously with his children about Lizzie's deteriorating condition.

By the time Jenny appeared, Joshua had pasted a calm demeanor on his face. Hugging her, he chatted a short few minutes and then made his exit. Not feeling like his usual sandwich in the quietness of his own home, Joshua headed toward the nearest fast food restaurant. Once in the drive through line, he studied the menu board, but nothing looked interesting. When an impatient driver blew his horn for him to hurry up, Joshua pulled forward and ordered a coffee with lots of cream. He then pointed the car toward his church.

Over the next hours, Joshua alternated between kneeling at the foot of the large wooden cross hung behind the pulpit area and sitting in the front pew reading the scriptures. Finally finding the peace he so desperately needed from the Lord Jesus and with a general idea of what to tell his children, Joshua rose to drive back to the hospital.

Once in his car he debated waiting until after supper when all his children would be there, but something pulled him to go now. Joshua checked his watch. It should be Seth's time with his mother. Deciding maybe the Lord wanted him to speak alone with Seth first for some reason, Joshua yielded to his strong need of touching the hand of his precious Lizzie and drove to the hospital.

Forty minutes later, Joshua stepped off the elevator on Liz's floor. His mind was preoccupied with Lizzie's deteriorating condition so it took a few steps down the hall before Joshua's attention was caught by the sounds of singing. Slowing his steps, he tried determining if it was a radio . . . or what. Progressing further down the hall, Joshua's eyebrows knit in a frown as he realized it was a-cappella voices and they appeared to be coming from his Liz's room.

Quickening his pace, Joshua moved toward her door when a nurse fell in step beside him.

"They've been at it for over half an hour. At first, we nurses thought to stop them, for other patients had begun buzzing for our attention; but to our surprise, the other patients were wanting us to open their doors wider, so they could hear better. They all asked us to let the singing continue."

Bewildered, Joshua asked, "But who? Who's singing . . . and why?"

"It's your children, Mr. Warner! Go see for yourself."

What Joshua saw as he peeked through a gap in the door brought quick tears to his eyes. Except for seeing the end of her bed, Elizabeth was out of his line of sight, but Joshua could easily see the backs of his three children. Jenny was snuggled in the middle between her brothers and they all had their arms draped around each other's shoulders and waists. As Joshua stood listening he heard the trio finishing up a very familiar Christian chorus called – **He's Able**.

As their voices quieted, Joshua heard Tony ask, "Do you two

remember Mom telling the story of how Jenny would sing 'He healed the smoken hearted' instead of the - brokenhearted?"

"Yah . . . I remember that," Seth replied.

While Jenny stated smugly, "I always was the cute one."

Joshua watched the three of them turn their focus back on their mother. Thinking he should make his presence known, he moved to go in when Jenny asked, "Do you guys remember the song Mom and Dad would sing at the graveside services? I think it was a song from scripture . . . something about peace."

Her question caused Joshua to pause. He waited to see if his boys knew the answer.

Tony spoke first. "I know it was from the Book of John in the New Testament, but I don't remember the exact verse."

To everyone's surprise, Seth quietly stated, "It was John 14:27."

Tony and Jenny swung surprised looks Seth's way.

"That's it!" Jenny exclaimed.

"Wow . . . how'd you remember that?" Tony asked.

Seth shrugged his shoulders. "I guess it's because peace was the one thing I struggled with the most. I never could seem to find it." He paused and then added, "Plus, there was something powerful about the way Mom and Dad sung it. They'd do it a-cappella while standing in front of grieving families who'd just lost a loved one. They were singing comfort and hope to those hurting people . . .

many times to people they didn't even know."

As Seth talked, Tony stepped out of Josh's sight. When he came back in view, Joshua saw an open Bible in his hands.

"Here's the verse," he said while holding it up to the others.

The three studied it a bit before Jenny asked, "Seth, do you by chance remember the tune? I'd really like to sing it to Mom."

"Sorry, sis, I don't."

There's my cue, Joshua thought. Pushing the door open, he walked in while softly singing, "*Peace I leave with you, my peace I give unto you...*"

The three of them swiveled as one to face him with surprise and then delight on their faces. As Joshua kept singing, one by one the three joined in. Soon all four were holding hands facing Elizabeth . . . singing.

"*Not as the world giveth give I on to you, not as the world giveth give I on to you. Let not your heart be troubled, neither let it be afraid, peace I leave with you, my peace I give unto you.*"

When the song drew to a close, Joshua turned to his children . . . whose faces had tears coursing down them. For a moment he couldn't speak over the lump of love he felt for each one. Clearing it once and then twice, Joshua finally found his voice. Asking them to walk with him further away from the bed, Joshua solemnly stated, "Kids . . . we need to talk."

A second later he saw the nurse from the hall softly step in, reach for the door knob, and then quietly walk back out . . . shutting it behind her.

~ ~ ~ ~ ~ ~ ~ ~ ~ ~ ~

Joshua was so proud of his children.

The talk had been difficult and honest, but not really a surprise to them. When it was all said and done, Joshua suggested it was time they all started getting on with their lives. Jenny emphatically stated, "Dad, my place is here right now. If we need to move Mom to a nursing home, I plan to stay until such time as I know she's stable."

Tony's only comment was to say that he'd help look for a nice place for his mother.

At that point, it was natural for all to focus on Seth who appeared to be studying the floor. The group waited and when he raised his eyes, Seth said, "Dad, I've decided to find a job in this area. Would it be okay if I moved back home . . . at least, until I'm able to get on my feet enough to find my own apartment?"

"Of course, son. Wherever your belongings are let's get them here. You're more than welcome to stay with me . . . err . . . your mother and me, for as long as you'd like."

"Ummm . . . may I say something?" Tony suddenly asked.

Once he had their attention, Tony focused on his brother. "Well . . . I was wondering . . . what I mean to say is . . ."

Seeing his family members all raising their eyebrows at his hesitating words, Tony took a deep breath and as it exhaled he blurted, "I have a two bedroom apartment, and well . . . the other bedroom is just setting there gathering junk." He then finished with, "Why not move in with me?"

The group was stunned at Tony's words, especially Seth. He glanced with wonder at his dad and sister before asking, "Are you serious?"

Tony stepped up to his younger brother and placed a hand on his shoulder. "I think it's long overdue for the two of us to spend more time getting to know each other better, don't you?"

"I do!" Seth responded incredulously. "I'd love that!"

The words were no sooner out of his mouth, when the old Tony seemed to rear up to say carelessly with a shrug of his shoulders, "Besides, if it doesn't work I can always ship you off to Dad's."

Immediately Seth's eyes grew large at his brother's flippant words. He started to back out of the deal when Tony surprised them all again by wrapping Seth in a bear hug to say, "Just teasing you, bro. This will be great!"

After that the four of them had left Liz's room to go eat supper in the cafeteria. It was their first time of leaving her completely alone during the supper hour, but Joshua thought it was important to stay together.

Upon their return, they were surprised to find that things had been done to Elizabeth in their absence. Someone had come in and repositioned her body. The nurse still standing by the bed explained, "Due to Mrs. Warner being comatose and not moving, the doctor is concerned about her circulation, especially on the side with the casts. He wanted to help relieve the stress on her body and back, so he ordered us to set up the bars above her bed and elevate her whole right side."

Elizabeth's right arm was shooting straight up to the ceiling while being supported by a type of sling around her wrist; her right leg was also suspended from the upper bar in a sling. The whole process pulled Elizabeth's body more onto her left side and off her spine altogether.

The foursome stared as the nurse continued. "The new position should help with circulation on her right side and eliminate fear of bedsores on her back."

Then making sure all adjustments and slings were secure, the nurse asked if there were any questions. Not receiving any, she left the room.

A short time later, the kids had kissed their mom good night and had also left.

Now Joshua was alone with his beloved.

Strangely restless, he paced the room a few minutes, finally coming to a stop at Liz's side. Studying her new position more intently, an idea began forming in his mind. Before implementing his plan, he made sure the door was securely shut, then walked back to the bed and lowered the nearest railing. Pulling his own casted arm as far left as he could, Joshua slowly got on the bed beside Lizzie. Careful not to disturb the ventilator or IV connected to her left hand, he got as close as he could then lovingly placed his left hand on her abdomen.

Not knowing how much time he had and with his mouth close to her ear, Joshua began talking.

"Hi, sweetheart. I hope you don't mind, but I needed to feel your body next to mine."

There was so much he wanted to say, but at that moment what came to mind was a trip they'd taken as summer missionaries to Puebla, Mexico when their children were still in elementary school.

They'd spent the night in a school dormitory located in the mountains. Very early that next morning, Joshua had woken his family up to follow him out a back window and up a fire escape ladder to the roof. The five of them had sat there in the early dawn watching the sun rise.

"Do you remember, Lizzie, the breathtaking view we had that early morning in Puebla, Mexico? It was amazing! Once the sun started coming up, we could see the outline of two peaks in the distance. It was like they jutted out of the plateau the city was on, from out of nowhere."

Breathing warmly on her ear, Joshua whispered, "Sweetie, do you remember how we felt at the discovery that we were actually staring at a snowcapped volcano? It was so awesome that we began praising the Lord Jesus for the wonder of His magnificent creations. What a time we had, huh Lizzie?"

Joshua's voice trailed off as he vividly remembered the scene and the profound love he had felt at that moment for his Lord Jesus Christ, his children, and Lizzie in particular.

Then a song suddenly came to mind; one that Lizzie often played on the CD player in the kitchen. As the words would float around the house, Liz often came to find Joshua . . . she wanted to let him know how much the song spoke of her love for him.

Now lying quietly beside Lizzie, the words of "Endless Love" played out in his mind as Joshua softly hummed the tune in her ear.

'My love . . . there's only you in my life . . . the only thing that's bright. My first love . . . you're every breath that I take . . . you're every step I make . . . And I . . . I want to share all my love with you . . . no one else will do . . . And your eyes . . . they tell me how much you care . . . Oh, yes, you will always be . . .My Endless Love.'

Silent tears rolled on to Elizabeth's sheet as Joshua choked out the last three words.

Then, giving way to his love for her and his despair over her condition, Joshua cried himself to sleep.

~ ~ ~ ~ ~ ~ ~ ~ ~ ~ ~

Sometime later, the night nurse nudged Joshua to say it was time he went home.

Gently unwrapping himself from her side, Joshua rubbed his nose on hers and then went home. Strangely, once in his own bed, he expected to have a hard time going back to sleep, but instead he slept soundly.

The next morning, Joshua marveled at how rested he felt as he walked down the hall to Elizabeth's room. At her door, Joshua moved to step in when it opened and the doctor stepped out.

He seemed momentarily startled at Joshua's presence, but then said, "Mr. Warner we ran an electroencephalography, known as an EEG, on your wife this morning. I'm very sorry to tell you . . . but the line was flat."

Noting the blank look on Joshua's face, the doctor went on to gently explain, "That means her brain has stopped functioning. It looks like your wife is brain dead, Mr. Warner."

CHAPTER TWENTY-THREE

(Somewhere in Time)

"Puebla, Mexico! I can't believe we're really here!" Elizabeth English excitedly stated to her fiancé, Joshua Warner. The two of them stood with a group of short term missionaries. The plan was to do street evangelism with some veteran missionaries in Puebla and other towns spread throughout the mountains surrounding Mexico City, starting the next morning.

Due to low cloud cover, the group hadn't been able to get even a glimpse of the majestic mountain peaks which ran the length of Mexico, Central America, and South America - - the rugged Andes.

Puebla, Mexico sported an Evangelical Bible Institute which would serve as the group's base over the next ten days. Once the rooms had been assigned and luggage unpacked, the young men and women congregated in the chapel before heading to bed. Once prayer was done, the leaders again went over the strict guidelines as to male and female interaction. It had been a really long day's drive from the City of Monterrey so most of them had only sleep on their minds.

That is . . . all except, Joshua Warner.

He was still too wound-up. In spite of the dismal, rainy climate Joshua could see how old and unique the building being used as a dormitory was – not to mention the sheer size of it. Once all was quiet, he had plans of sneaking around to explore as much of it as he could before getting caught.

As he walked Elizabeth toward the room she was sharing with three other women, she yawned heavily. Earlier he'd tried talking her into sneaking out to go with him, but Elizabeth had stated she was too tired.

At the door, he discreetly glanced around before quickly pecking her on the cheek and squeezing her hand. "Sleep well, my love. See you in the morning."

Slipping through the door, she admonished, "Get some sleep, Josh. We have a big day tomorrow and remember . . . we're at a higher altitude so we'll get tired more quickly."

"Will do," Joshua assured while grinning from ear to ear.

Yah, right! Liz thought as she closed the door.

It seemed she'd no sooner fallen asleep when someone gently, but insistently nudged her awake. It took Liz a moment to remember where she was. When her eyes were fully open she was startled to find Josh's face very close to hers. With a finger for silence, he beckoned her to get up and come follow him. He was obviously very excited.

He handed Liz a robe from the foot of her bed, and then turned his back while she threw back the covers and tied the robe on. When the knot was secure, she slipped her hand into his. Joshua then led her tiptoeing out of the room, while keeping an eye on her sleeping roommates. Once he verified the hall was clear, they walked out. While Joshua carefully shut the door, Liz leaned in close to his ear to demand, "What's going on?"

Josh whirled around to face her. When he did their lips almost met. For a moment time seemed suspended, until Josh pulled his head back. With a broad smile he stated, "I have something to show you, but we have to climb on to the roof. Are you game?"

Liz studied the face of the man she loved and nodded.

"Great! It's this way."

So saying, Joshua lead her to a nearby window and slowly raised it. Once he had climbed out, he leaned back in to quietly explain, "There's a ladder here leading to the roof. I'm going to back down it a bit so you'll have room to climb up ahead of me. Be careful."

He then disappeared.

Liz swung her legs out the window and soon found herself standing on a small ledge near the ladder. For a moment her rash decision to follow him pummeled her when Elizabeth stared down at the ground three floors below.

"Don't look down!" Joshua urged as he came back up the ladder. He guided her onto the ladder and then the two made their way to the roof. In short order the two were standing on a flat part between two metal roof peaks.

"Okay, now you really have to trust me, Lizzie. I want you to close your eyes. I will then guide you to a special sitting position before you can open them. Can you do that for me?"

Elizabeth loved doing these adventures with her Joshua. From past experiences, she knew there had to be something really special he wanted her to see. Pausing a moment, she stared straight up into the sky. A gasp escaped at the myriad of stars she saw dancing in the night sky. The cloud cover had lifted.

"Are you ready?" Joshua asked as he took her hand once more.

Closing her eyes, Liz drily observed, "We are so going to get into trouble for this."

She heard a smile in Josh's voice as he began moving her forward. "Probably, but it's worth it!"

A short time later, after a few bumps and "sorrys" he backed her into some kind of alcove which cut off the cool air wafting around them. Sitting her gently down, he then slipped in beside her. Putting his arm around her shoulders, Joshua said with awe, "You can look now. Open your eyes."

Until that moment, Elizabeth hadn't realized just what time it was getting to be; but when she opened her eyes a kaleidoscope of sights assailed her senses and she was stunned into silence.

There before her was a flat plain stretching for miles in the distance and right in the middle were twin snowcapped peaks with the sun just starting to peak out behind them at the base.

Liz sucked in a gasp and slowly exhaled. "It's so-o-o-o beautiful! Are those volcanoes?"

"I believe one of them is."

Joshua sat there proud as a peacock while darting his eyes back and forth from her expressive face to the panoramic view spread out before them. The two were silent; drinking it all in. No words could express the majesty and wonder of God's creation.

Involuntarily, Liz began humming "Amazing Grace" while coming to her feet. She wanted to see beyond the limits of the two metal peaks. Slowly she pivoted on her heels until she'd done a full circle and was facing Joshua once more. "Thank you for bringing me up here. It's wonderful."

Still seated, Joshua softly replied, "You're welcome. There's not any other person I'd rather share it with. After all, you are my . . ." Josh's words stopped as a frown knit his brow. Looking past Liz's head, he stared with confusion toward something up in the sky.

As she watched a look of absolute horror filled his face.

That prompted Elizabeth to turn and look up also. What she saw confused her. It was a giant hook descending out of the sky . . . it appeared to be coming down from Heaven.

Joshua leapt to his feet grabbing for her, but the hook suddenly became two hooks; one latched onto Elizabeth's right wrist; the other around her right ankle. It then began to slowly lift her sideways off the roof.

He lunged for her free hand, but missed, almost falling off the roof in the process.

Pure terror coursed through Elizabeth as her whole body was now off the roof and she stared helplessly down. "Josh! What's happening? Josh?"

Slowly, she felt herself being reeled up backward faster and faster toward Heaven and away from her Joshua.

Consumed with fear, Elizabeth began screaming his name over and over and over again - - - before all went black!

~ ~ ~ ~ ~ ~ ~ ~ ~ ~ ~

After the doctor's devastating news, Joshua called his children back to the hospital. A short time later another EEG was done . . . this time with Joshua and his children nearby.

To their dismay, the results were the same.

Afterward, the doctor took them to an empty room across the hall and shut the door. "Mr. Warner, I know this is a sensitive topic, but are you aware of your wife's wishes under these circumstances?"

"Yes, I am. As a matter of fact, I'm the one who asked my daughter to bring in Elizabeth's signed paperwork for your records."

The doctor acknowledged Joshua's words with a nod, then opened a folder he'd been carrying under his arm.

"Good. Just so I know all of us are on the same page, I'm going to read aloud her wishes so the others will know also."

With that, he then read the document portion giving Joshua full authority to make decisions on Elizabeth's behalf in the event she were unable to participate in the medical treatment decisions.

"Having read that . . . I believe, Mr. Warner, that we've arrived at a decision point as to whether the patient should be left on the ventilator or not. I understand this is an extremely difficult decision, but I'm going to need your answer some time fairly soon."

The doctor then took a long moment to study each face before exiting the room.

Unaware he'd been holding his breath during the doctor's speech; Joshua suddenly exhaled heavily and then sucked in fresh air before meeting the eyes of his children.

"I know the final say is mine, but I'm interested in your

thoughts."

The three stared at their father, but remained silent.

"Well then, should we all spend a few moments alone and then talk?"

This time Seth spoke up. "Do you really think any of us are going to have any easier time deciding if we're alone rather than together?"

"No . . . no, I don't" Joshua fell silent before saying, "Okay, let's try this again. Tony . . . what are your thoughts?"

Tony ran a slightly shaking hand through his hair while clearing his throat. "The test showed no brainwaves twice now. If the machine may be the only thing keeping Mom alive, I say . . . I say . . . we need to shut it off."

Once the words were delivered, Tony sucked in a gasping breath and hurried from the room.

The remaining three stared at the newly opened and closed door.

"Jenny?" Joshua softly said. "What do you think, honey?"

"Dad," she replied while tears spilled down her cheeks. "We all know that Mom wouldn't want us to keep her here under these circumstances. She'd want us to let her go be with the Lord Jesus."

With that, Jenny threw herself into her father's one good arm and sobbed.

Over her shoulder, Joshua's own brimming eyes stared into the equally wet ones of his youngest son.

"Seth?"

"Dad, we're all assuming the machine is keeping Mom alive. Maybe it's not . . . maybe the EEG is wrong! Maybe her brainwave is slow enough that the machine can't pick it up!"

Seth rubbed his cheek and eyes with his hands. Sighing he added, "I've just gotten my life right with the Lord Jesus Christ and it's important that I start trusting Him. . . that includes in the area of what's best for Mom. We all need to do that." He paused a long moment and then added with a catch in his throat, "Dad, we need to shut it off and trust God with the results."

Opening his good arm, Joshua beckoned his son closer.

"You're right, son . . . and, I believe we need to tell the doctor that we're ready now."

At his words, Jenny lifted her head. "Dad, we need to find Tony first. We should all be there together."

"Of course, sweetheart; let's go find him."

Joshua released both of them, but before he could reach the door to open it, Jenny grabbed his arm.

"Dad, I just remembered something! A few years back there was this young man injured in an accident out west somewhere. Anyway, the EEG tests showed no brainwaves and he was pronounced officially dead."

As Jenny talked her words became more excited and rushed.

"The family had gathered to say their good-byes when one of his cousins felt a strong impulse to run his pocket knife along the bottom of the dead man's foot. When he did the foot twitched. It happened fast but several saw the movement, so a family member ran to get the doctor. When he came in, the doctor took the pocket knife and pricked the body under one of his fingernails. According to the article I read, at that point the young man's eyes came open. He recovered, went home less than a week later, and even appeared on some of the TV talk shows!"

Finished with her story, Jenny fell suddenly silent and breathless.

Joshua stared lovingly at his daughter. "Jenny, honey . . . with God all things are possible, but we also need to remember that it just might be time for your mother to be with Jesus in Heaven. Plus . . . I'm not sure where you're going with this story. Do you want me to pull out my pocket knife and try it on your mother's foot?"

"I'm not sure what I want. Or . . . maybe I just want you to be open in case Mom shows any signs, however slight, that she might still be trying to get back to us."

"Jenny, I promise that if anything surfaces, I'll help your mother the best I can. Now, let's go find Tony."

Meanwhile, after he'd made his declaration, Tony had

needed to grab fresh air. The family found him leaning against his car in the parking lot, so the four of them gathered there to talk quietly about the decision made. They then held hands while Joshua led in prayer . . . committing the outcome into their Heavenly Father's all powerful hands.

CHAPTER TWENTY-FOUR

(Still Somewhere in Time)

Elizabeth squinted at the bright sun peeking its head from behind the snowcapped volcanoes in the distance and her soul filled with peace and love. Squeezing Joshua's hand she closed her eyes to revel in the moment.

Then a chill hit her and Liz's eyes flew wide open. She stared in bewilderment at the scene laid out before her.

She was no longer standing on a roof top holding her beloved Joshua's hand. Instead she was standing in a field of tall grass and Joshua was no longer there.

Elizabeth was alone . . . and confused.

Suddenly . . . dark clouds began swirling above her and the wind whipped the grass at her ankles. A sense of fear crept up her back, and . . . the urge to run.

I need to find Joshua!

Elizabeth frantically searched for him. She ran here and there, but couldn't find him anywhere. As the sky continued to darken, Liz felt more fear and confusion over what was happening. Spying some trees in the distance, she angled toward them . . . all the while screaming Joshua's name.

As she moved closer to the trees, Liz noticed the grass was taller and thicker. It slowed her progress. Soon, like tentacles the grass began entangling itself around her right ankle. Liz struggled to reach the safety of the trees as panic threatened to overcome her!

Then the grass turned into vines climbing up her right leg and then trapping her right arm. The vine began pulling her skyward.

Giving in to utter despair, Elizabeth slowly floated backwards into nothing while screaming, "Joshua, where are you?"

Then . . . in a hopeless tone Elizabeth whispered, "I can't find you!"

~ ~ ~ ~ ~ ~ ~ ~ ~ ~ ~

After the doctor was notified of the family's decision, he took them once again into the empty room across the hall from Elizabeth's. He wanted to brief them on what to expect. When he was sure they all understood, the doctor explained why an RN was qualified to do the shutting off, but that he'd be in the vicinity if needed. He also stated that the heart monitor would be left hooked up to give an accurate reading of Elizabeth's heart beats.

Solemnly the family followed the nurse back into Elizabeth's room. Once all were inside and the door had closed, she stepped aside allowing the family time to say final words to their loved one.

Joshua, Tony, Jennifer, and Seth stood holding hands around Elizabeth . . . not saying a word, just staring wide-eyed at her motionless, comatose body. Then one-by-one each broke from the pack to kiss her cheek and say private words in her ear. Removing themselves a short distance away, the three kids gave their father time alone with Elizabeth.

A long moment later, a red-eyed Joshua straightened to turn toward his equally red-eyed children. Three nods told him they were as ready as they'd ever be. Joshua pulled a chair up close to the bed so he could hold Lizzie's hand, and then he did one of the hardest things he'd ever had to do . . . he signaled the nurse to shut off the ventilator machine.

When the ominous click of the shut-off hit his ears, Joshua flinched; but his eyes remained glued to Lizzie's dear face, as did all the others in the room.

A sense of dread and hopelessness lay heavy on the family members as they tensely waited.

~ ~ ~ ~ ~ ~ ~ ~ ~ ~

Once again, Elizabeth found herself back on the roof in Puebla, Mexico; only this time her focus wasn't on the volcano, it was on a bright light high above her head . . . a light that appeared to be coming toward her. Elizabeth was fascinated with it, and wondered if Joshua was seeing it too. She turned to ask what he thought it was, but found he wasn't there. Temporarily forgetting the bright light, Elizabeth stood to search the roof peaks, but no Joshua.

Meanwhile, the light drew ever closer. And yet, for some strange reason that fact didn't bring fear to her.

But Joshua's missing presence did!

Elizabeth's brows knit into a frown at Joshua's sudden disappearance. Still ignoring the light above, she began calling his name. When no reply came, fear grew within her which prompted Elizabeth to begin yelling Joshua's name. Sensing the light still coming closer, Elizabeth continued ignoring it as she cautiously edged to the ladder and peered down.

Still . . . no Joshua.

Where is he? Why can't I find him? She wondered.

"Joshua . . . where are you?" she hollered out loud.

Again . . . no response.

Then something even stranger happened.

A sunbeam ray came down from the light, covering Elizabeth like a warm blanket. The warmth felt just like a giant hand of love wrapping itself around Elizabeth's whole being – body, soul, and spirit.

Her anxiety over Joshua's absence became replaced with wonder at the awesome way the light was making her feel. Then, Elizabeth's ears picked up sounds – of several voices. She turned one ear skyward, but wasn't able to distinguish any individual sound for certain.

Not only was the bright light above, it was now totally surrounding her. It so engulfed her with love and peace that Elizabeth forgot her concern for the missing Joshua. All she could think about was the light and wanting to give herself to it – forever.

Involuntarily, her arms spread wide as she tried to pull the light closer. Elizabeth felt as if every part of her was being consumed and pulled into the light.

Elizabeth smiled . . . for she was ready to join the light.

The light swirled around her and Elizabeth began laughing. She felt lighter than air. Closing her eyes, she began whirling around and around in joy while saying over and over, "Lord Jesus, is that you? I'm ready, Lord."

~ ~ ~ ~ ~ ~ ~ ~ ~ ~

Joshua jumped when an alarm sounded near his head. At the same time, Elizabeth's body began twitching and jerking on the bed. Not sure what to do, Joshua glanced at the heart monitor machine. It showed that her heart was racing. He turned toward the nurse with a question in his eyes.

At the same time, the nurse rushed forward with a syringe in her hand.

Instantly, Jenny darted forward to grab the nurse's arm while pleading, "Dad?"

Joshua stared deeply into his daughter's eyes. He remembered the story of the young injured man and how the machines had been wrong; and he knew what his daughter was asking.

Standing, he stepped in front of the nurse. "What are you planning to do?"

"I'm going to make this easier for your wife and sedate her! Now, please step aside and have your daughter turn me loose!"

Again Jenny spoke, "Dad, Mom may be trying to come back to us. She needs more time!"

To which Seth urgently added, "If Mom's sedated we might hinder that and lose her for good."

For a split second Joshua wrestled with the issues at hand. That is until the nurse moved to go around him, then he stated firmly, "Leave her be!"

"I can't Mr. Warner. It's inhuman! She needs . . ."

"I said leave her be. Give her a chance. What harm can it really do?"

"But, Mr. Warner . . .!" The nurse stared at the family

closing in on her, before angrily stating, "I have a duty to this patient!"

Right then another voice sounded from the doorway. "Nurse, you heard them. Leave her be."

The nurse stared at the doctor standing there, and then in a huff of disagreement removed herself to the far end of the room.

As she did, the family's focus swung back to Elizabeth's face. Her whole body tensed as Joshua leaned close to her ear.

"Lizzie, we're here. Are you trying to come back to us? Come on, baby, try! You can do it!"

Elizabeth's body grew very still . . . motionless once more.

All eyes darted to the heart monitor. The previously racing heart beat was slowing.

The family members didn't know whether to have hope or be alarmed as with eyes darting between Elizabeth and the machine they circled her bed.

~ ~ ~ ~ ~ ~ ~ ~ ~ ~ ~

Elizabeth continued standing with her arms spread wide while staring upward into the bright, beautiful, peaceful light - with her mouth open and laughter bubbling out.

Then an even more bizarre thing happened.

Another beam of light separated itself out and shot into Elizabeth's open mouth and down her throat. Once inside, it burst into a million beams.

The sensation was so startling that Elizabeth arched her back to begin taking in huge gulps of air. She felt like her heart was trying to leap right out of her chest.

~ ~ ~ ~ ~ ~ ~ ~ ~ ~

Silent tears streamed down the four faces of Elizabeth's loved ones, as they willed her to come back to them.

Then the heart monitor sounded its bell once more. Elizabeth's heart rate was climbing again at a rapid rate. At the same time, her body stiffened as she arched her back.

Not able to handle it any longer, Joshua moved his face over hers. In a loud voice he commanded, "Elizabeth Warner, it's time you came back to us! I need you! We all need you! You have to fight! Don't give up! You can do this! Open your eyes!"

~ ~ ~ ~ ~ ~ ~ ~ ~ ~

As Elizabeth soaked in the warmth of the light, it grew brighter and more intense. Then, out of the midst of the bright light a single voice spoke loud and clear; a voice that had Elizabeth's full attention.

She listened intently while trying to understand the words. At first she puzzled over the strangeness of the words, but then slowly clarity came and she knew whose voice it was.

It was her beloved Joshua . . . and he sounded upset . . . very upset.

Elizabeth frowned.

Why is he yelling at me like that? He shouldn't be yelling at me!

As she mulled that over, Elizabeth wondered where he'd been and how come he'd left her alone on the roof top.

Then, the light's power consumed her again and thoughts of Joshua disappeared.

But not for long . . . her beloved Joshua's voice called at her once more. As she strained to hear his voice, Elizabeth noticed that the light began pulling away from her. A part of Elizabeth wanted the light to stay, but another part of her began thinking that if the light lifted she'd be able to see her Joshua. She wanted to talk to him about the light and wondered if he was seeing it too.

As the powerful, warm light continued to move upward, Elizabeth looked up to watch it leave. It was so bright she had to close her eyes. When she did, it was then Elizabeth felt another, dimmer light just beyond her eyelids.

At the same time, Elizabeth felt a hand clasp hers.

A large, warm hand that felt good . . . and . . . right.

Then, as if he was standing beside her once more, Elizabeth heard her beloved Joshua's voice. "Lizzie, it's time to wake up now. We're all here waiting for you. Come on sweetheart, you can do it. The Lord Jesus says you're to come back to us for a while longer."

Not sure if she was still on the roof top, Elizabeth looked up to locate the bright light. It's moving away had made her anxious

Pamela Bush

and sad.

"Lord Jesus is that you? Are you leaving me?"

At her questions, the light stopped its movement as a very gentle, loving voice clearly said, "It's Me, my precious child. Your Joshua was temporarily lost to you, but now you need to listen to his voice. I still have more for you to do on earth. Your Joshua still needs you, your children need you, your grandchildren and all the other lives you will touch while still on the earth . . . need you. Elizabeth, open your eyes . . . it's time to wake up!"

Elizabeth Warner's smile faded as she stared at the light containing her Lord and Savior. She knew He was telling her it wasn't time for her to join Him yet. She also knew she needed to obey His command to wake up. Part of her wanted to obey, but most of her wanted to stay with the Lord.

"But, Lord Jesus, as much as I love Joshua and my precious children, I'd rather stay here with . . . wait . . . did you say . . . grandchildren?"

Filling with a sudden new urge to do as the Lord commanded, Elizabeth turned her head to face the dimmer light once more. She tried opening her eyes, but found everything too bright. Squinting, Elizabeth tried to shield her eyes, but found she was somehow restrained and couldn't move.

What on earth? What's going on?

Concentrating harder, she tried to figure out what was

231

happening. It was then she realized only one hand was restrained, the other was being held gently by a warm, large hand.

Fuzziness continued controlling her thinking processes, but another thing soon became clear – something was in her throat and covering her mouth.

That realization caused fear and panic to the forefront of Liz's mind; followed closely by a rush of adrenaline.

Something terrible is happening and I have to escape! Surged through her clearing mind as Elizabeth became intent on breaking free from whatever was restraining her. With all her strength, Elizabeth began thrashing and fighting the restraints. Her confusion multiplied when a chaos of voices sounded loudly around her awakening senses.

"Lizzie, stop! You'll hurt yourself! You must be calm!"

Then, "Tony keep her right side as steady as you can."

Other voices seeped into her waking consciousness.

"Mom, oh Mom, you're coming back to us."

"Maybe it's too bright in here. Can the lights be dimmed?"

"Good idea, Jenny. Go soften the lights, but not too dark. I want your Mom to see us when she opens her eyes."

"Nurse, give her something in the IV to calm her, but not to put her out!"

"Yes, doctor."

Strangely in all the noise and turning on of her senses,

Elizabeth could also distinctly hear another voice somewhere in the room quietly plead, "Jesus, please help Mom in this moment. Calm her heart. Help her to realize what's going on and where she is."

A firm hand held Liz down on her left shoulder while saying in an urgent voice, "Lizzie, lie still! It's me, Joshua! Please listen and stop fighting us!"

Finally, that voice punched through the clouds in Elizabeth's mind and she grew still . . . listening for him to speak again.

Aware that Liz had stopped thrashing and was possibly hearing his voice, Joshua softly said near her ear, "Liz, honey, I need you to open your eyes now. I'm here. The kids are here. We need you back with us now."

I know that voice. I can trust that voice. In that moment, Elizabeth felt strongly that she needed to obey.

Slowly, she pried her heavy eyes open as the familiar voice kept encouraging her to return to him and those who loved her.

Once her eyes were completely open, Elizabeth was acutely aware of being in a strange room full of people; of machines nearby making various noises, of tubes in her nose and mouth, of her whole right side jacked up in the air; but what literally held her complete attention were the warm hazel eyes she was staring deeply into.

She'd found her Joshua at last. Happiness swelled up within her as Liz tried shouting her heart to him the only way at the moment she could - through the means of her eyes.

Getting the message, Joshua in return wrapped her in a warm blanket of love overflowing from his own eyes.

In that moment, Elizabeth knew that whatever lay ahead everything was going to be alright. For a peace that surpasses all understanding filled Elizabeth's heart, mind, and soul as Joshua said, "Welcome back, Sweetheart. We missed you."

Pamela's First Non-fiction Novel

The story of her son, Paul's struggle with Crohn's disease and how it changed the lives of the whole family.

A story of how her son never gave up even during his most stressing times – physically, emotionally, spiritually ; and about his faithful wife, Gretchen who has stood by his side through good times and hard.

You can find out more about this book and Pam's other novels on her website – *pamelabushauthor.com* – where they can be purchased or you can purchase any of her books through amazon.com or order from any bookstore.

THE WHIRLWIND SERIES

Book One

Book Two

Book Three